LORRAIN

I live in Wiltshire with my husband but love to travel and have lived in four continents. From playing amidst Roman ruins in Africa as a child to riding a Sultan's racehorse in the Middle East as a teen, I've many experiences to draw on for the stories I've been writing ever since I can remember. When I'm not writing you'll find me listening to audiobooks while I sew or design handbags, usually with a rescue terrier or two curled up on my feet!

Secrets of a Chalet Girl

LORRAINE WILSON

Harper impulse

Harper*Impulse* an imprint of
HarperCollins*Publishers Ltd*
77–85 Fulham Palace Road
Hammersmith, London W6 8JB

www.harpercollins.co.uk

A Paperback Original 2014

First published in Great Britain in ebook format by HarperImpulse 2013

A catalogue record for this book
is available from the British Library

ISBN: 9780007559589

Automatically produced by Atomik ePublisher from Easypress

I'd like to say a big thank you to the lovely team at HarperImpulse and also to Maria and Dawn – thank you so much for your help with this book.

CHAPTER ONE

"Pick a Dare, Flora, it's your turn." Tash thrust the shiny, silver gift bag across the bar towards Flora.

Flora had assumed Tash brought the bag along from Chalet Repos because it contained an early wedding present for Holly, or more likely silly 'L' plates or even worse… she'd heard talk about inflatable costumes.

No such luck.

Even dressing up as an inflatable penis might be preferable to carrying out a dare Tash had made up.

"Um, I don't know..." Flora licked her lips nervously. Looking around at the group she could tell everyone was glad it wasn't their turn. Tash's wilder streak was enough to make anyone uneasy. She should've known Tash offering to take a hand in organising Holly's Hen night was a bad omen.

Really? They were playing some kind of Truth or Dare game? She'd played spin the bottle as a teenager. It never ended well.

It might have been better if Holly's best friend Pippa had been in charge of the plans. But she'd only arrived in Verbier this morning. Plus she had lively one-year old Lexie to keep her busy, so she was hardly in a party planning frame of mind.

Take a bunch of emotional girls, add in copious amounts of cocktails and play Truth or Dare… What could go wrong?

There'd be tears before bedtime. Hopefully not hers.

Her skin prickled with the awareness she was being watched by the other bar customers. It was the third Verbier bar in their bar crawl this evening. The fact they were wearing dresses in a resort town where everyone wore salopettes by day and jeans, albeit designer ones, by night, had already attracted them a fair amount of attention. Holly insisted they dress up, saying she never got a chance to be 'girly' nowadays.

"Come on Flora, get on with it." Sophie giggled, signalling to the barman that they needed more drinks. Her shiny mane of blonde hair and baby blue eyes, coupled with a dress that revealed an impressive cleavage meant they'd had no trouble getting served.

Feeling self-conscious in her silky blue evening dress, Flora shifted uncomfortably on her barstool and hoped she wasn't going to humiliate herself in public.

Ha! Dream on…

"You should just be glad you don't have to do the chalet girl initiation thing I went through." Holly grimaced sympathetically.

"Me too, she's right, you should count yourself lucky." Sophie laughed. "The initiation was you had to go to Wonderbar, take your bra off and flash the crowd. Although some we could mention fudged it."

Sophie winked at Holly, smirking but Flora couldn't join in the laughter, panic now rising about what she might have to do. Her face flamed with heat. She hated blushing, always had ever since she'd been teased at school for her ability to turn scarlet so easily.

"How do you know I haven't put that Dare in the bag?" Tash winked and practically thrust the shiny silver bag under Flora's nose.

I am so not taking my bra off and flashing the crowd. No. Not. Not!

"I'd really, rather not. I mean I couldn't…" She faltered.

Bloody Tash.

Flora caught Holly's eye, pleading silently '*Help me.*'

"We won't make you strip, I promise," Holly interrupted, placing a hand on Flora's elbow.

Flora exhaled slowly with relief and smiled gratefully at her boss. *Rescued!*

Holly was lovely like that. Not to mention great to work for given she'd actually been doing the job herself last season and wasn't afraid to muck in when they needed help.

Maybe she was paranoid but it felt like everyone in the packed bar was staring at them. A quick glance confirmed most of them were. Now Flora wished she hadn't worn her high heeled boots and been persuaded into wearing her silky midnight blue dress. Right now she might as well be wearing a sign over her neck saying she was on the pull.

Do I want to be on the pull? It might be a good distraction and I certainly need one of those.

That would probably be the Dare, knowing Tash. Ever since she'd found out Flora hadn't had sex since coming out of a long-term relationship she'd been on at her to get back in the game. Or had it been 'on' the game? With Tash you never really knew. She liked to shock people.

The group of men closest to them sniggered. She was sure she heard them assessing the hen party girls, picking their favourites and giving marks out of ten. She seethed quietly, skin burning as she swallowed down her irritation. Only one of the men here had caught her attention when they walked in and he wasn't even looking over at them, his attention purely on his mobile phone.

"Okay, I'll do Dare then," she said crossly, gulping her cocktail and trying to force a smile to her face for Holly's sake. It was Holly's night after all. Sophie and Amelia were playing along with Tash's stupid game, which meant she had no choice…

It was going to be a long night.

She tried to keep the smile in place as she pulled a card out of the bag. Sophie and Tash cheered.

'Kiss the sexiest man in the room.' Fantastic! Not much better than having to flash a crowd.

Flora bit her lip as the girls grabbed the card before she could toss it back in the bag and pick again. Why couldn't she have picked a drinking challenge involving cocktails? Now that was a Dare she wouldn't mind.

She caught Holly's eye, trying to smile but her cheeks ached with the effort. She didn't want to be a buzzkill. Pippa looked shattered and had made it clear she hated leaving baby Lexie in Steve and Scott's hands for the evening but she was making an effort. As for the others, well, you couldn't share a room with three other girls and not realise fitting in wasn't just preferable, it was a matter of survival.

"I'll need another Mojito if I'm going to do it," she squeezed her eyes shut.

You can do this Flora, pretend you're in a film. Act the part. You came to Verbier to have fun so how about you fricking well get on with it?

The Mojitos and Cosmopolitans consumed so far this evening certainly helped.

I was supposed to get married tomorrow.

I need another cocktail.

"So, who is the sexiest man in the room?" Sophie spoke too loudly, swivelling round on her bar stool and almost falling off. Holly laughed, putting an arm behind Sophie's back to steady her.

The stocky barman winked at them as he served their drinks but Flora's mind flickered instantly to the gorgeous looking man still glued to his BlackBerry. Apart from the whole phone addiction thing, something about him initiated warm stirrings in parts she'd thought had iced over permanently.

She hadn't been able to properly put him out of her mind since they'd arrived. He'd been on his own, leaning nonchalantly against the bar, focused on his phone and looking very scrumptious. When he sensed her checking him out, he'd looked up and given her the sexiest smile she'd ever seen. His eyes were a rich dark blue and they crinkled at the corner when he smiled. It was then she'd felt that… not-at-all-unpleasant stirring thing…

Instead of maintaining eye contact he'd gone straight back to his BlackBerry, so maybe he hadn't felt what she had if his phone was a bigger draw than she was in her sexiest dress.

So, kissing that guy had its attractions. But walking up to him and kissing him without any prelude? She needed to be a hell of a lot drunker than she was.

Although, I could always just kiss him on the cheek like I'm greeting him and then claim mistaken identity.

As excuses went it was so lame it needed a walking stick. But in the absence of any other plan it was going to have to do.

"I think she already has someone in mind," Sophie slurred. "What fun."

Flora guessed she'd seen the involuntary flutter of her eyes towards the end of the bar and cursed herself for being so easy to read.

People who know you this well should be banned. Or at least banned from giving you stupid Dares.

This was what came from sharing a small dorm room. You all got to know each other way too well…

"How old are we?" Flora rolled her eyes, trying to look dignified but fearing she resembled a nervous horse.

"It might be fun," Holly said, smiling at her. "You might even enjoy it. And it's better than having to take your bra off in public, trust me!"

Tash narrowed her eyes at Flora. "You must make it a proper snog. No pecks on the cheek allowed. If you fluff it we'll make you do the Wonderbar Dare instead."

Flora shuddered; she knew Tash meant business.

Mental note to self – don't let Tash anywhere near my hen party preparations.

Not that she planned on getting married.

Ever.

Oh sod it. She was delaying the inevitable. It was only a kiss for goodness sake. Time to woman up. She took a quick sip of the cocktail that'd appeared in front of her – Sex on the Beach instead of the Mojito she'd asked for. Maybe it was an omen. Not that there were many beaches around here, except if you counted the lake shore beaches.

Stop faffing about, Flora.

"Okay, I'm doing it," Flora announced, and the girls whooped in unison as she clambered carefully off her bar stool. Falling flat on her face and flashing her knickers would not be a good look.

To cheers of "Go Flora," she made her way through the crowd to the end of the bar, clutching the velvet strap of the beaded evening bag she'd designed herself tightly, more for something to hold onto than anything else. Inexplicably she couldn't remember what to do with her hands when she walked.

She had a prickling sixth sense feeling she was being watched. Oh yes, that would be because she *was* being watched.

Nice evening Holly. I'm here to celebrate you getting married by making a complete tit of myself. Nice.

Her mouth felt dry and her brain woolly as her target came into view. He was still texting on his phone.

A quick in and out, before he knows what's hit him. Then a very swift exit from the bar…

Before she could move he looked up and they both stared, a flash of connection passing between them. It felt like the world around her was melting away, leaving only her and BlackBerry guy in the bar.

He smiled again, a devastating smile. She froze, fear and adrenalin pulsing through her, competing for control.

Go now. Quick. It's only a kiss!

Only a kiss? Huh. And he was *only* the sexiest man in the room. *And* the girls were all watching her.

So, no pressure then.

Someone shrieked behind her and Flora looked back to see Sophie, Amelia and Tash falling about laughing, clutching each other like schoolgirls. They would pay for this. Pippa and Holly were also smiling but in a 'sorry it's you but glad it's not us' way.

They clearly weren't sympathetic enough to save her.

Was this what all bar hook-ups were like? Perhaps there was some kind of special code she should know about? Who knew, one raised eyebrow and you might accidentally agree to re-enact 'Fifty Shades of Grey'!

You're acting remember, just do it!

She closed the gap between them, hands trembling as she leant forward towards him, rising up on tiptoe so she could whisper in his ear. She desperately hoped he spoke English. The vast majority of Verbier residents did, to her surprise. Her French wasn't up to more than ordering food or asking where the loos were. It hadn't been an issue up until now given Scott only marketed Chalet Repos in the UK.

The scent of him momentarily distracted her; it was citrusy, clean and masculine.

Concentrate Flora!

"I'm really sorry but I'm afraid I have to kiss you," she whispered in his ear, aware of how close their bodies were. "I promise you I'll go away immediately afterwards."

Then she sent her inhibitions flying and went for it, meaning to kiss his cheek and sod what Tash said but instead BlackBerry man turned his head and kissed her fully on the lips. Before she could register the feel of his lips on hers he was tasting her and teasing her and her lips responded to him, obediently, unthinkingly… it felt like she was falling down into another world – Flora in Wonderland.

Christ, she really was actually falling. The guy had dipped her backwards, firmly supporting her back as he leant in for a deeper kiss. Her parted her lips with his tongue and her mouth welcomed him instinctively, wanting to say yes to whatever he asked.

It felt strange. Strange and wonderful.

Not to mention that this was a hell of a lot more than she

bargained for. Her skin fizzed and the attraction hit her like a body blow. She'd thought these kinds of kisses only existed in the movies. Something deep inside her melted, mellowing her, her inner romantic responding to this stranger against her conscious will, issuing him an invitation.

Her inner romantic was clearly a tart.

In her dim awareness of what was going on in the background she heard wolf whistles. One of them sounded very much like Tash. It hauled her back to reality with a sudden lurch.

Bloody hell. I'm in a ski resort bar with an audience. This has to stop.

She tried to struggle upright. Instantly he helped her up, drawing back a little but his face remained close to hers, dark blue eyes locked on her in a way that sent darts of anticipatory desire zinging through her body. The air between them fairly crackled with sexual electricity. Every nerve ending tingled.

Wow.

Six months without sex could clearly send a girl a bit loopy.

"Hi, I'm Zac Hengler, and you are?" His tone was as cool as though they'd simply bumped into each other, not shared *that kiss*, the kiss she was still reeling from.

"Um, Flora," she replied, feeling dazed and disorientated.

"Umflora?" He grinned wolfishly. "Unusual name."

"Umflora Lyndon." Despite her mortification Flora's lips creased into an automatic smile, joining in his joke, her body determined to give this guy the green light no matter what she did.

"I don't usually do this, honestly. I'm sorry." She shrugged, wishing she couldn't still inhale the clean, citrus scent of his aftershave, that it didn't make her want to bury her head against his chest.

Down girl!

"No need to apologise. So you're English? Only an English girl would do that and then apologise." Zac grinned.

"I'm not, I just had to…" Everything was coming out wrong,

her tongue not connecting properly to her brain. "We're playing Truth or Dare. Really silly I know. It wasn't my idea."

"Oh, I don't know, I think it sounds like fun. Can I play?" Zac smiled a slow sexy smile and Flora's insides gave a delicious lurch as though she'd been thrown into the air by a fairground ride – the Supersonic Swooner.

Who needs a fairground ride with Zac around?

Her cheeks flamed even hotter and she became intensely aware of Zac's hand still resting on the small of her back. What would it feel like if those fingers dipped lower, stroking and touching… She took a tentative step back, confused, her desire to run battling her inner hussy's craving to offer herself up to Zac on a plate.

Don't you dare! Single for a year remember? You've got to stop handing control over to men.

"I don't want you to get the wrong idea about me," she said, not even sure what the 'right idea' was. Her physical reaction to Zac shocked her.

"And what would that be? That you're attracted to me?" His eyes held her gaze, challenging her. "So, tell me the truth, what made you pick me?"

There was more than a hint of arrogance in his sexy smile and it stirred Flora's fighting spirit. She'd had her fill of arrogant men and had no compunction about putting them in their place.

"You looked bored," she replied, shrugging. "And I thought maybe you'd been stood up from the way you keep checking your phone, so I felt sorry for you. Er, at least I assume you're here alone. Oh God, you haven't got a wife or girlfriend have you? I really should have thought…"

She bit her lip, how could she have been so stupid.

I'm never drinking Mojitos ever again.

"Relax." He laid a hand on her bare arm and another bolt of sexual electricity shot through her. Her eyes widened and she stifled a gasp.

How does he do that?

"No girlfriend, no wife," he confirmed. "Since you're asking."

"Good." She exhaled loudly with relief. "I mean I'm glad I haven't caused any problems, not… I wasn't asking because of…"

Shut up Flora!

She fell silent and shrugged, shaking her head at her ineptness.

"And you?" Zac's eyes shone with amusement but beneath that she sensed something more serious – a magnetic tug, pulling her towards him. Pulling her into him. Part of her wanted to plunge right in, to jump instead of tentatively dipping her toe in at the edge of the shore.

Sod paddling, she wanted to swim.

"No boyfriend, no husband," she confirmed, looking him directly in the eye. "And I'm not looking for either."

Zac raised his eyebrows and grinned cockily. She narrowed her eyes at him.

Great, Flora, what did you have to give him a challenge for? Everyone knows there's nothing like being unavailable to increase your attractiveness.

His dark blue eyes shone with an intensity that made her shiver. It was desire, she recognised it in him because she felt it too. Its re-emergence after so long shocked her. It had evolved; this new, ravenous desire was nothing like the old.

It had grown up, and so had she.

"But you didn't answer my question," he reminded her.

Question? What question?

"I don't remember…" It was hard enough remembering her own name right now, never mind keeping track of the conversation.

At any rate the words passing between them didn't seem to matter a whole lot. Hundreds of messages had already flashed between them, in their eyes, their body language, the skin on skin touch of his fingers lightly holding her wrist and in the current of sexual electricity she couldn't ignore.

Why am I fighting this? Why should I ignore it?

This was a near perfect set up if she wanted sex but no

commitment – a foreign country with a gorgeous man she might never have to see again after tonight. Wasn't it about time? Verbier was about breaking free, kicking back and having some fun.

Right now she had the power to say yes or to walk away. She was in control and that felt good after all the crap she'd had to deal with back home.

If I can't be bold now when can I be? It's time Flora. Just go for it…

She was aware of the hen party girls closing in en masse behind her. The drunken giggling was a bit of a giveaway. They'd obviously decided she'd had enough space for one evening.

Please piss off!

She sent them furious telepathic signals but they weren't picking up. Great.

"Hi Flora, if you want to stay that's fine but we thought we'd head back to Chalet Repos." Holly touched her lightly on the elbow. "Pippa's worried that Scott and Steve will've dropped baby Lexie in the Jacuzzi or something. Hey Zac, you look in better shape than Scott after the Stag Do. I heard last night got pretty wild."

Flora realised she was still in physical contact with Zac and pulled her hand away swiftly. So Scott and Holly knew Zac? While reassured on one level he wasn't an axe-wielding psycho, part of her wanted Zac to be a total stranger, to stay a total stranger. That he was friends with her bosses made her a little… uneasy.

"Perhaps I should come back with you." Flora wavered, her fingers tightening on the velvet bag strap, the sensible part of her trying to control her inner hussy. This wasn't exactly something she'd done before. Getting it together with a random stranger in a bar was what other people did, not her. But so much had changed recently. How could she even be sure who she was or what she wanted? After years of Tom telling her what to do, the freedom to make her own choices felt… weird.

It was a nice kind of weird, though.

Verbier was a start over, a blank page just waiting for her to write in it. She couldn't sit around waiting for someone else to come along and write her story for her. She'd already been there and done that in the first volume of 'Flora's Life.'

Volume two was going to be very different.

There's nothing wrong with having sex for pleasure. It's about time you bloody got some!

"Hey, you stay. It's fine, you're on leave until the wedding remember, no guests to get up for in the morning. I'd make the most of it if I were you!" Holly smiled, linking arms with an anxious-looking Pippa as they walked to the exit. "Don't do anything I wouldn't do."

If I were you… So that's pretty much the green light from my boss then.

"That doesn't leave much," Tash shouted back to Holly, winking at Flora in an exaggerated way. The girls fell about laughing and Flora waited for the ground to open up and swallow her whole. Well why not? It felt like the kind of evening where anything might happen.

When she wasn't magically transported away from the scene Flora risked catching Zac's eye and a lurch of desire jolted her, her insides performing a loop the loop, leaving her physically shaken. But as powerful as the desire was, a little niggle buzzed at the back of her mind like an annoying insect.

"Excuse me for a moment Zac."

She took a few steps towards Tash, reaching her before she got to the exit.

"Did you set me up?" she whispered furiously in Tash's ear. She could feel Zac's eyes on her from where he stood at the bar. They trailed over her body, over the fabric cupping her breasts, lingering on her legs… she didn't know how she could sense it but the sexual chemistry in the air felt palpable.

It feels like magic.

She shivered again, half with desire and half with fear. She had a choice – go back to the chalet and get ribbed by the girls for being a coward, not to mention spending a sleepless night burning with frustration. Or she could stay here with Zac and let this go further.

Her body screamed an instant 'Stay!'

"You haven't been laid in six months Flora," Tash hissed back, a little too loudly in Flora's opinion.

"Great, shout it a little louder would you, I think there was a guy over in the far corner who didn't quite catch that," Flora muttered, her jaw clenching and molars grinding. "Thanks a bundle for making me sound desperate."

Breaking up with Tom had been so bloody traumatic, especially with all the hassle she'd been given afterwards about calling off their wedding. Leaping into bed with someone else hadn't been top of her to-do list given she'd suddenly had nowhere to live, no job and oh yes, had been the most hated girl in town.

"Let me see the Dare bag," Flora asked, a suspicion occurring to her. She made a lunge for the bag and managed to grab it. She opened card after card.

Each one read 'Kiss the sexiest man in the room'

"Did you switch the bag?"

Tash shrugged unrepentantly. "That's what friends are for. I made some spare cards in case you needed a little push to get back out there. These ones were for you. So what? Have fun, you deserve it and you'll be thanking me in the morning."

Sophie lurched in the direction of the barman and Tash grabbed her arm, knocking the cards out of Flora's hands in the process.

"Amelia and I will get her back safe safely. Seriously Flora you need some fun, it's way overdue." Tash put on her stern, 'don't mess with me face' that worked so well on the chalet guests who thought it was funny to pinch her bum.

That was true at least.

Could I?

As the possibilities fluttered into her mind her attitude softened towards Tash. Tash knew how hard her last relationship had been, how traumatic ending it had been for her. She didn't know all the details, but she knew enough. They'd all talked long into the night about their love lives on more than one occasion.

If I can't have fun here in Verbier when is it going to happen?

It's time.

Zac bent down for one of the cards that'd fallen to the ground before Flora could stop him.

Shit.

His eyebrows shot up and he grinned. "So, I'm the sexiest man in the room am I?"

Flora's face flamed again. She cursed her inability to stop blushing, really she should have grown out of the habit by now, she was twenty-four for frick's sake.

"Well, the bar's a bit short of talent tonight," she replied stiffly.

There was nothing worse than a gorgeous man who knew exactly how sexy he was. That knowing smile was irritating and annoyingly… attractive.

Damn.

He laughed and took her hand, tugging her back towards the bar. She went unresistingly, aware of the gentle but insistent pressure of his other hand at the small of her back. The force of his will seemed sufficient to drive her but a part of her rebelled against this assumption of control.

After all, Tom had assumed control so slowly, so subtly at first that she'd thought she was imagining it and over-reacting.

These kinds of charms often acted as a mask and who knew what lay beneath?

I'll just have to be careful.

"I'm all for you doing what the card says." He lowered his mouth to hers and before she knew it they were kissing again. Her body pressed so firmly against his it was as though they were magnetised, relentlessly and ferociously drawn to each other.

She forgot the girls, even forgot she was angry as her fears melted away with the heat of his kisses. When he eventually pulled away the room seemed to spin a little. Her mouth opened but no words came out.

"Shall we get some fresh air?" he asked.

She nodded and averted her gaze from the smug smile of the barman. She had to see where this might take her. And she really, really needed to have sex. It'd been too long and her wakening senses demanded satisfaction.

"Why don't we continue Truth or Dare back at my chalet?" Zac's arm snaked behind her, his fingers lightly caressing the small of her back through the silk fabric of her dress, making her skin tingle in a very nice way. "It sounds entertaining and it could be much more fun in private."

A thrill ran through Flora's body and she pushed her anxieties to the back of her mind where they hovered, buzzing at her like insects, just present enough to be annoying.

I need to lighten up.

"It would sure beat holding Sophie's hair back at two in the morning." She joked, stalling for time, not making a move towards the coat rack at the door. If she left with him there would only be one outcome tonight.

What would sleeping with a man like Zac be like?

Only one way to find out.

She'd been with Tom since…well, it felt like forever. It actually *had* been forever. She'd never had sex with anyone other than Tom; that couldn't be normal.

If she could find out what it felt like with someone who really knew what they were doing, just once…

Her body screamed at her to go anywhere this man asked her, to do anything he asked. Only the tiny trickle of fear running down her spine kept her feet from moving. She could hear Tash in her head, berating her and telling her she didn't deserve this chance if she was going to be a wuss.

Aren't you supposed to feel the fear and do it anyway?

"I promise you, if you spend the night with me it will be a hell of a lot better than the alternative you described." Zac murmured in her ear, his stubble lightly grazing the side of her cheek.

"Oh really?" She laughed, looking down at her new boots. From now on they were going to be her lucky boots. "It doesn't exactly set the bar very high does it?"

"Are you okay?"

That he sounded curious, not scornful or impatient made her like him even more. Her weird behaviour hadn't sent him running for the exit yet and she was sure with his sexy smile he could have his pick of the girls in this bar or any of the other Verbier bars for that matter.

"Erm..." She fiddled with her bag strap, picking at a loose thread and absently thinking she must do something about it. "It's just I don't really know you, it feels a little…Well it's not something I'm used to doing, you know?"

She looked pleadingly at him, willing him to understand she was inexperienced and not dismiss her for being totally pathetic.

"If you're worried I'm about to kidnap you, you don't need to be. Let's see, I'm a respectable management consultant with a flat in Geneva and a chalet here in Verbier. I love to snowboard. What else? Well, I'm quite fond of après ski and I like sex."

"Right. Your English is very good but I can definitely hear something else in your accent?" She tried not to react to his mention of sex.

Great, now you sound like you're making conversation at a church garden party! Not sexy Flora.

"My father's Swiss," Zac's smile tightened. "Hence the Swiss surname. But I was sent to boarding school in England and my mother's English."

"Okay." Flora's tense muscles relaxed as she nestled against his firm torso. She could feel the hard muscle through his shirt, was aware of her flesh responding to him, her nipples hardening on contact.

I want this. I need this.

"So you're happy to come back with me now you know my mother's English?" He teased.

"Sort of, it's nice to know a little about you."

"And how about you Umflora? What do I need to know about you?"

"Absolutely nothing." Flora giggled. It was great being able to finally say what she liked and do what she wanted. This was the first time since leaving Tom she felt really free from him, free from home, free from the old Flora…

"I promise I'll come up with much more interesting Dares. Because if you don't want to tell me anything you'll have to do what I dare you to."

"And vice versa, you'll have to do what I dare you too," she countered, feeling playful and liking the idea of having some power.

"I look forward to it." Zac leant in closer and planted a soft kiss on her neck. She shivered, certain they both knew Zac was way more experienced than her. What would he say if he knew she'd only ever slept with one man?

I do hope he doesn't ask me that.

Come to think of it there were all sorts of things she hoped he wouldn't ask her. It would be so much nicer if he did things to her instead.

"Relax." Zac stroked her ribs through her dress, sending sparks of desire ricocheting throughout her body. "Let's go, shall we?"

CHAPTER TWO

Like there'd ever been any doubt about whether Flora was going to leave the bar with Zac. She'd been kidding herself that she could walk out of this bar and take the turning back for Chalet Repos at any time but she knew, deep down, there was only one place she was going.

To bed with Zac.

She went with him to the coat rack and once he'd helped her into her coat they stepped out onto the street. The icy mountain air assaulted them immediately. Flora shivered, half with the cold, half with anticipation.

She glanced up at the dark, star-strewn sky. It seemed appropriate; as she walked along the street with Zac's arm behind her back, steadying her on the icy patches of pavement, it felt like taking a step into the vast unknown.

She was due some adventure.

Playing Truth or Dare made it easier. After all at least fifty per cent of the time she would be in control. There was quite a lot she wanted to ask Zac about himself. Getting to know him might be a lot of fun.

And then there was the sex…

"Is it far?" she asked.

"It's just up here, the modern chalet with the large windows."

He pointed to a snow-covered chalet further up the hill ahead. It nestled up above the town centre, facing the magnificent drop down over the Val de Bagnes and the view across to the French Alps. It was a sight that usually took her breath away but tonight she only had headspace for Zac.

At least his chalet wasn't as flashy or as large as some of its neighbours. It was a relatively new building, a quirky design but built with the same wood as the traditional luxury chalets surrounding it. The front of Zac's chalet had windows the height of the building facing the mountain view and a couple of balconies to sit out on to enjoy the Swiss sunshine during the day and stars by night.

Nerves hit her as they entered the main cabin. It was cosy with large padded dark leather sofas contrasting with light oak flooring. The splashes of colour in the room came from the books on the shelves that covered an entire wall of the room. The volume of books impressed Flora. It was kind of nice to find another reader. Not that it mattered obviously. This was only going to be a short-term fling so it hardly mattered if they had much to talk about.

Zac walked over to the log basket by the fireplace and tossed another log onto the still smouldering fire. It hissed in protest and then sent flames licking around the new source of fuel, flaring into life. Outside in the darkness, snowflakes began to fall, slowly at first, then growing ever larger until the night sky was thick with snow, giving it an eerily pale glow.

"Drink?" he asked.

"Erm, I probably shouldn't."

Shouldn't drink and probably shouldn't be here. Oh help, what have I got myself into?

"Can I tempt you with a Kir Royale?"

"Okay," she folded, mentally swatting the worry-insects away. "You've found my weakness."

A couple of sips wouldn't do any harm. It might help her to relax. She wouldn't finish it. On top of the cocktails she'd already had, it could be lethal. Or at the very least, it could lead to her doing or saying something she'd regret.

"I hope to find a lot more weaknesses," he replied, the corners of his mouth twitching. "It will save me a lot of time if you tell me up front."

"You'll have to work a bit harder at interrogation than that," she said, taking the tall champagne flute filled with rich, dark-pink bubbles. She sipped at it, the fruity blackcurrant bursting onto her taste buds before she swallowed. The warmth spread through her chest like a comforting embrace, relaxing her.

Zac knows what he's doing. He does this a lot.

Somehow the thought of Zac bringing numerous different women back to his chalet after a day on the slopes didn't disturb her as much as she'd thought it would. It helped her to feel anonymous. It would be as though she'd never been here. Maybe Zac wouldn't even remember her. That thought gave her a kind of freedom. It didn't matter how bad she was in bed if he was going to forget her.

After tonight, apart from the wedding, maybe she wouldn't have to see Zac again if she didn't want to?

Perfect.

Tash was right. This was the best way to leap back into the dating fray – with a sexy stranger in a foreign country. If she screwed up who would know? No strings sex – absolutely no pressure.

She felt peculiarly light-headed, whether it was from the Kir Royale or the feeling of freedom and anticipation pulsing through her body she wasn't sure.

Probably a little of both.

"Come and sit down," Zac patted the leather sofa next to him and she approached cautiously, perching on the edge a little further away than he'd patted.

Zac took some dice from a drawer in a lamp table and selected one.

"Let's play Truth, Dare or Forfeit," he announced. "If you throw a one or a two that means a Truth, three or four mean a Dare and five or six will be a Forfeit – the thrower has to forfeit an item of clothing of the other player's choice."

Flora's stomach fluttered and her skin prickled to attention. Zac was so impossibly handsome – a strong jaw shadowed with stubble, intense dark-blue eyes and a physique an athlete would be proud of. He looked like he could wrestle a bear without breaking sweat. Hmm, where had that come from?

If he'd suggested playing naked Twister she would've agreed. Now there was a thought...

She wouldn't mind telling him to take off his shirt either. As soon as he threw a five or a six it was coming off.

"Forfeit was never part of the deal," she protested, not wanting to seem too eager, too easy...

It's a bit late for that.

"My chalet, my rules." He grinned and raised an eyebrow, sipping at his Kir Royale but never taking his eyes off of her.

"But you're wearing a lot more items of clothing than me."

His eyes skimmed appreciatively over the lines of her silk dress, lightly hugging her curves. Heat burned her cheeks.

Damn, he was doing it again, making her blush. Heat spread through her body, desire flaring into life as its flames licked at her, teasing her...

He pulled his v-neck jumper over his head and threw it to the floor. "There you go."

The neckline at the top of his T-shirt revealed tanned flesh and a small amount of chest hair. She really hoped he'd throw a five or a six. She wanted to see what lay beneath that shirt, to lay a hand on his chest and trail it down his body...

It felt like a need rather than a want.

"Ladies first," he grinned, his firm thigh resting, seemingly casually, against her leg where she sat on the sofa. Had he moved or had she? Perhaps this magnetic pull affecting her really was strong enough to move mountains. Or bodies come to that. She was intensely aware of the warmth of his flesh at point of contact.

All her attention focused on the point where their bodies met, it was hard to think of anything else.

He handed her one of the dice.

She threw it onto the coffee table, only breaking off eye contact with Zac to see what she'd thrown.

A six. Great. Maybe she could take off her necklace or a shoe?

"I say you forfeit your knickers." Zac's eyes gleamed and Flora's stomach preformed an undignified back flip. Her fingers trembled as she threaded them together in her lap.

"Shouldn't they be last to you know… come off," she asked.

"You don't get to choose," he replied.

A thrill ran through her body at his words but still she didn't want him to know how much he was turning her on.

Hold back Flora. You have to hold back.

"Do you need a hand?" He added, mouth twisting with amusement.

The sod. He's enjoying my discomfort.

"No," she replied, wanting to be the girl who could take this in her stride. She'd come here for sex after all. This was no big deal. She didn't have to act coyly to hold back from Zac, there were many more ways to withhold herself emotionally and taking control was one of them.

Yet no one had passed on the boldness memo to her body. Her hands continued to tremble as they inched the hem of her dress up her body. She watched his eyes darken as they took in her hold ups and the bare flash of flesh at the top of her thighs. Hearing Zac's sudden intake of breath she parted her legs to give him a better view. She felt powerful.

She felt sexy and could barely breathe as she edged her knickers down and threw them to the floor, pulling the hem of her dress quickly back down as she did, only giving him the briefest of flashes.

"Your turn," she said, thrusting the dice at him to move the attention away from her.

He tore his eyes away from where her knickers lay on the floor and threw a two. Truth.

"How many women have you slept with, Zac?" she asked.

"I've lost count." His eyes danced, amused.

She gulped. They lived in different worlds, that was clear. But did it have to matter? She'd only been with the one man because she'd met Tom when she was seventeen and a virgin. Casual sex on Zac's scale was something she could only imagine. Would it feel different with him?

"Does it bother you?" he asked her, reaching over to lightly stroke the fabric of her dress where it covered her thigh, his touch rucked the dress hem up her body, seemingly accidentally.

Yeah right!

But she let it stay where it was and squirmed in her seat a little. "No, it should mean you're good at it by now. If you've had all that practice."

He threw his head back and laughed.

"So, will you give me marks out of ten?" he teased, his hand still languorously stroking her thigh in a way that drove her wild, the hem riding higher and higher until the lace of one of her hold-ups could be seen.

The fire in the hearth flickered, the flames licking the new log. Every muscle tensed, her body on high alert.

Hurriedly she picked up the dice and threw again.

"A four?" Zac's face lit up with a wide, sexy grin. "Now, what shall I get you to do?"

Flora's heart beat faster. She could feel the heat burning between her legs where she was growing wet. Her breasts ached to be touched.

Sexual desire; she'd almost forgotten what it felt like.

"Let me look at you," he said simply, removing his hand from her thigh.

"What do you mean, you are looking at me." She frowned, thinking it an odd request.

"I mean I want to *look* at you." He lowered his eyes to the hem of her skirt. "Lift up your dress, let me see you."

"Oh." She took a deep breath, her cheeks burning with embarrassment but doing what he asked felt strangely erotic. She pulled her dress up higher, slowly, teasingly, getting into character and emboldened by both the Kir Royale and the sense that none of this was really real.

Zac placed one hand on each of her ankles, taking her by surprise, lifting both her legs up onto his lap, gently parting them.

"Oh," she gasped.

Her skirt was now up around her waist and she was very, very turned on. She tuned in to the sensation of his fingers on her limbs, guiding her, seducing her. But his fingers travelled no higher than her ankles. He caressed her with his stare instead, and she found she loved the attention. Wanting him to do more drove her crazy but at the same time she found the build up of sexual tension erotic and empowering. The embarrassment faded away leaving pure lust.

The need for him to touch her swelled inside, powerful and insistent.

No one had ever stared at her in this way, or made her feel so sexually attractive. She wouldn't complain if he abandoned the game right now to make love to her.

The frustration of waiting for him to do something swelled inside her until she thought she'd burst. After a moment that seemed to stretch out forever Zac tore his eyes away and coolly picked up the dice.

She leant forward again, loosely tugging her dress back down again as she watched him throw.

"A six, I'll be having that shirt, mister." She sat up so she could get a better view, her fingers itching to tear the shirt from him and never mind the buttons.

She could feel sexual desire coiling tighter and tighter inside her with every inch of flesh revealed. His chest was firm and the muscles defined. The dark chest hair snaked down into the waistband of his jeans and she couldn't help letting her eyes trail lower to the obvious bulge of a large erection.

Good. So she'd made an impression then. It was always good for the ego.

Tash was right. This is fun and it has been far too long.

At the thought of the girls back at Chalet Repos she wavered, a part of her missing the familiarity of their nightly routine. The late night chats in the dorm room clasping mugs of hot chocolate were a world away from this. But that was the coward in her speaking. It was time to stop playing it safe.

And how often did a girl get this kind of offer? She locked eyes with Zac and knew with certainty wild horses couldn't drag her back to Chalet Repos; she was kidding herself. Perhaps she *had* to kid herself to feel she could walk away if she wanted to.

She needed an out, an emergency exit, just in case…

"Er, whose turn is it?" She blinked.

"Yours." He handed her the dice and his fingers brushed hers. A delicious tightening sensation tingled deep in the pit of her stomach.

"A one. Now what shall I ask you Flora?" He observed her thoughtfully. The only sound in the room came from the crackling fire.

Her heart beat faster, for some reason Truth felt scarier than Dare or Forfeit.

"I know, tell me where I have to kiss you to really turn you on."

Flora blinked hard. "Um, on my neck maybe."

"Maybe? You're sure that's the place that will really turn you on? I think we might have to test this to find out if you're telling the truth."

He pulled her across onto his lap and lowered his lips to her neck, caressing her skin with his lips. She moaned, her response out of control, her body automatically taking over as liquid heat pooled between her legs. Control rapidly disappeared as a viable option.

She could feel his erection beneath her dress and instinctively rubbed herself against him, wanting to push him out of control too.

Zac exhaled loudly, growing harder beneath her.

"Well, it works okay but I think I have to kiss you in some other places to test if that's really the best spot. How else will I know if you're telling me the truth?"

His hand slid up her thigh beneath her skirt, taking her by surprise as his fingers touched her clit. She jumped, startled at the touch, then she closed her eyes, giving herself over to the sensation.

He dipped his fingers inside her and she welcomed his touch. It had been so long…

"Oh, that's erm…" She squirmed and adjusted her position so he could get better access.

"You see if I kissed you just here." His thumb caressed her clit, sending sparks of pleasure through her body. "Well I think it might turn you on even more. Or we could try up here…"

With his other hand he stroked the swell of her breasts, lightly teasing her through the fabric covering her now protruding nipples, stiffening to his touch. Flora wanted his hands and tongue everywhere, wanted him to well and truly make love to her until every longing was satisfied.

The intense arousal felt almost unbearable. She was ready for him and wanted him inside her like, now! She needed him to touch her, explore her and bring her release.

She ignored the part of her still protesting this was all too fast. It wasn't making love – this was arousal. Pure lust. They didn't even know each other. It just felt like they did because the chemistry was so hot.

Her body might need the release, craving freedom, but her mind hung back, suspending judgement. It was like she was both prisoner and guard. Her sexuality sought freedom from the sentence of repression she'd imposed upon it. She stood, key in lock, trying to find the courage to turn it.

Fear surged inside her, so tangible it felt physical. The last time she'd made love it'd been… hideous. Tom had been furious with her for some reason, she couldn't remember why now, forgetting to pick his shirts up from the dry-cleaners perhaps, or not doing the washing up, who knew? In those last few months he'd been permanently angry, using sex to make her submit to him. Using it to remind her of his superior strength.

Why the heck am I thinking about Tom? He's not ruining this for me. I have to speed things up.

The memory of why she'd imposed a man-free zone on her body cast its long shadow over her. She had to claw back some control, to get on with this before she talked herself into wimping out.

She grabbed the dice and thrust it into Zac's hand.

"Your turn again," she struggled to catch her breath.

"Okay," he replied softly, fixing a curious eye on her as he threw the dice into the lap of her hastily pulled down dress.

It was a two. She thought hard before speaking.

I need to know more about this man.

"Who were you supposed to meet tonight? I saw you kept checking your phone. Did you get stood up? Were you lying when you said you didn't have a girlfriend?"

"Whoa, hold on. That's a lot more than one question." He looked her straight in the eye. "First off I don't lie, ever. That's not the kind of guy I am. I promise I'll always be upfront with you. As to your other question – my best friend Nick was supposed to be meeting me but he stood me up because his wife went into labour. They're both in the hospital in Martigny with my brand new godson, Tomas, born about an hour ago."

It wasn't what she'd been expecting to hear and it threw her momentarily.

"Oh, I see." Had she been wrong-footed? It was only fair she double-checked he wasn't spoken for, wasn't it?

"Does that satisfy your curiosity? Were you hoping a girl had stood me up? Because I have to say I've never had it happen yet;

have you ever been stood up?"

"I don't have to answer you, I'm not the one who threw a two," she replied haughtily, pulling her legs up underneath her, curling up on the seat beside him.

No, of course he'd never been stood up. That only ever happened to mere mortals.

"I believe it's your throw," Zac said, retrieving the dice from where they'd fallen to the floor. He placed one hand on her thigh as he handed it to her and her flesh responded eagerly to his touch. She wanted to give in with abandon, really she did but…

Would she ever be free of Tom's shadow, darkening everything she did? She'd had enough of it. It was ridiculous, why should he get to spoil sex for her indefinitely? If she let thoughts of him intrude and ruin tonight then he was still winning.

I can't let him win.

She leant against Zac's warm body to indicate she was still interested, aware she'd been giving him as many mixed signals as a malfunctioning traffic light. Maybe he'd think she was playing hard to get?

She threw a six.

"The dress." Zac raised an eyebrow, clearly expecting some objections. His sexy smile made her stomach flip over.

She'd show him.

Sod it!

Zac was gorgeous and this was happening. She took a deep breath and reached behind her back to the zip but her fingers trembled, fumbling with a fastening that stubbornly refused to yield.

"Let me." Zac leant forward, his mouth close to her ear as he reached for the zip, his fingers brushing her skin as he pushed her hair aside. She turned her back to him to make it easier. When he pressed his lips to the nape of her neck she almost leapt off the seat. The kiss was so hot it felt like he'd branded her. She shuddered, the air escaping her lungs with a sudden rush. When she'd said she liked her neck kissed she'd chosen it because it was a safe option, she hadn't realised it could really feel this sexy.

Gently, slowly he tugged down the zip and the dress fell away. She expected him to touch her or kiss her again. She wanted him to trail kisses down her spine to the small of her back; she was particularly sensitive there.

He did nothing. And it drove her wild. She needed his touch, her skin craved him.

She turned to see his eyes, dark with desire as they focused on her with a sensuous intensity, drinking her in. They lowered to her breasts, still covered by a pale pink lacy bra and they stayed there a while, lingering appreciatively.

The attention was intoxicating, as was knowing that he liked what he saw from the bulge in his jeans.

It'd been a long time since anyone had looked at her like that. It was amazing how easily her confidence had been eroded. It had been a slow drip, drip into her psyche until one day she'd finally woken up a victim and knew she had to build her own life raft or drown.

No more, stop thinking about the past.

Then her eyes locked with Zac's and she felt so connected to him, so totally and utterly drawn to him that at that moment, rightly or wrongly, she would have trusted him with her life. And right now she trusted he would give her the shag of her life.

"Your turn mister," she said, smiling as she tossed him the dice.

He threw a four.

Flora considered, her heart beating wildly in her chest. She knew what she needed to ask. She summoned all her courage, aided by the desire fizzing through her veins like effervescent sherbet.

"Make love to me," she said.

CHAPTER THREE

Zac raised his eyebrows, studying her carefully, probably deciding whether to torture her a little more before giving her any kind of release.

She knew it wasn't really making love. It was sex, but she couldn't bring herself to ask him to shag her and the 'f' word felt too brazen, even for a girl dressed only in a pink bra, hold-ups and high-heeled boots.

"It's an official Dare, I need you to… make love to me," she said as boldly as she could, leaning back on the sofa and wondering if she dared go as far as to part her legs in invitation.

Hmm, maybe not. "Please?"

That's right Flora, you may as well beg. You've lost your clothes; you may as well shed your self-respect along with them.

In reply, Zac tugged at the button fly of his jeans, quickly getting rid of the rest of his clothes. Flora watched with interest as he revealed his long muscular thighs. The bulge in his black trunks told her how turned on he was.

Very.

That makes two of us.

He rose up from the sofa, taking her hand and pulling her up towards the fireplace, stopping on a cosy faux-fur rug.

"Take off your bra and lie down."

She wanted to protest that he wasn't giving the orders but as though second-guessing her he put a finger to her lips. "You asked me to make love to you, so trust me and let me do it my way. I promise you'll enjoy it."

It was an arrogant assumption but she believed him. She was so turned on he'd barely have to touch her to make her come. She swallowed down her embarrassment as she undid the clasp of her bra, letting it fall to the ground. She was aroused, more aroused than she could ever remember feeling and it helped that, at this moment at least, her desire was stronger than her fear.

Zac pulled her down onto the rug and lay next to her, propped up on one elbow so he could look at her. Flora wished they were still playing Truth or Dare. This felt too serious, the flirty edge had gone. She didn't need a barometer to tell her the atmosphere was heavy with sexual tension. She felt connected, almost too connected to Zac.

This wasn't supposed to mean anything.

A tiny flicker of panic licked at her, the contradictions confusing her. How could she feel two opposing emotions so strongly? Which should she trust?

"Come here," Zac edged closer until their bodies were touching, skin on skin and nose to nose.

Tentatively, shyly she reached out a hand to stroke his torso, parting her lips to meet his sensuous kisses, trying to let her body take over, responding to him instinctively. He seemed to understand she needed to start this slowly and somehow knew exactly where to stroke her and how much pressure to apply.

Gradually her shyness faded away as the burning swell of sexual desire rose up to overwhelm her. The kisses became more urgent, more frantic as their fingers explored each others' bodies. She reached down in between their bodies to stroke the erection that had been pressing hard into her thigh. Zac jerked away, his breathing ragged.

"Wait," he said. "There's no rush. First I want to find out if you were telling me the truth."

She frowned. The truth about what? For the briefest of moments it flashed through her mind that he somehow knew about the mess she'd left behind at home in England.

Don't be ridiculous Flora!

"I mean the truth about where I have to kiss you to really turn you on." He rolled over, pressing his lips to her neck. "Is it here you said you liked it?"

"Hmm," Flora replied absently, enjoying his lips against her skin and inhaling his clean, citrus scent. Zac smelt so good.

"Or should I go down a bit lower?" he whispered, trailing a line of kisses down to her breasts. She gasped when he took a nipple in his mouth and sucked hard, almost bucking off the soft rug.

He raised his head and looked directly at her, eyes dark with promise. "Or should I go even lower?"

The breath caught in her chest as she wondered where he'd kiss her next, half wanting it, half afraid of the intimacy.

"No." The word was out of her mouth before she knew it. She tried to smile to soften the harshness of her response, thinking quickly. "I want you inside me now. Please don't make me wait. Do you have, you know… protection?"

Her cheeks flared hot and it wasn't because of their proximity to the fire. Great, she was really messing this up. So far she'd ordered him to make love to her and told him to get on with it. Of course Zac had protection; he did this all the time. At least, despite a quizzical look on his face, he didn't say anything to make her feel even more awkward. She was grateful for that at least.

"You okay Flora?" he asked, once he'd fetched the foil packet from a convenient drawer.

"Sure," she replied, smiling at him. "Sorry Zac, it's just been a long time since I…"

"It's okay, no need to apologise. No need to explain either if you'd rather not." He sat down next to her. "We don't even have to have sex if you really don't want to."

"But I do want to," Flora replied, feeling dangerously close to tears.

He cupped her face and kissed her and she let the melting sensation take over again.

No thinking.

She reached out to stroke his erection, needing him to know she really did want this.

"Kneel down," he whispered in her ear, nibbling her earlobe gently. "If you go on all fours I can touch you while I'm inside you, we can come together."

She shivered, feeling feverish with need, want and nerves, letting him place her in position, allowing him to pull her legs further apart, exposing her sex to him. She waited, wet and aching for him to be inside her and heard the rip of the foil packet. Once sheathed he pressed himself against her, rock-hard against her. His arm reached round to tease her clit, rubbing it rhythmically until she thought she'd explode.

She pushed back to meet him as he entered her. She heard a moan and realised it had come from her lips. Zac's ragged breathing was a turn on and it helped she wasn't staring into his eyes, feeling his questions. It was easier to let go. She pushed back against him, meeting his thrusts. His fingers continued to stroke and tease, his other hand holding her hip. She was lost to the sensation, to every movement, feeling they were moving in perfect time, dancing to the tune he was playing with his fingers.

And so did Zac. He expertly tipped her over the edge, helping her reach her climax. Pleasure pierced her, rippling through her body, making her contract around him. Almost instantly he tensed and jerked inside her, before he came.

She'd been right.

Zac was fantastic at sex.

When Zac returned from the bathroom he found Flora sitting, staring pensively into the fire. It'd been a strange night. His best friend was now a father and last night had been Scott's Stag Do. Everyone around him was moving on and the ghost of Christmas present had loomed its ugly head. He was pretty sure he wasn't welcome back home for Christmas drinks this year. And he still hadn't asked anyone to be his date for Scott and Holly's wedding yet. He'd had a different plus one for each of his friends' weddings so far.

Maybe Flora would be free to be his date. Spending more time with her sounded… nice. There was something so natural about her, a distinct lack of artifice he liked.

"Okay?" he asked, touching Flora lightly on the shoulder to alert her to his presence. She jumped in alarm then composed herself quickly, but he'd seen the flash of panic in her eyes.

There was definitely a story there. That brief flash of insecurity made him feel protective. Vulnerability always did.

Tonight has been a big deal for her.

"Shall we get into bed? It'd be much warmer. The snow's getting heavy out there. Hopefully there'll be a nice covering on the slopes tomorrow. Do you snowboard?"

She shook her head. "I prefer to ski, I think it gives you more control."

"I could teach you if you like? I hear you've got some time off – isn't Chalet Repos filling up with family and guests for the wedding? Just like Scott to block out two of his busiest weeks to satisfy Holly's romantic whim."

"I'm good thanks, I'm quite happy skiing, I don't need…" she blushed as she got to her feet and followed him into the bedroom.

Cute.

He loved how easily she blushed.

"I think it's lovely, Scott and Holly getting married on New Year's Eve – the anniversary of their first kiss." She climbed into the bed, quickly covering herself with the Egyptian cotton duvet and disappearing down into it so he could only see the tip of her nose and top of her head poking out.

"I thought you didn't do romantic." He climbed in beside her.

"I didn't say that, I meant, well…"

"Well you said you didn't want a boyfriend or a husband," he replied. "And I'm assuming that after what we've just done you didn't mean you were looking for a girlfriend instead."

"Well, no, of course I didn't mean that," she squeaked, pulling the duvet completely over her head, muffling her voice. "Can't you behave like a stereotypical male and go to sleep?"

"Hey." Zac reached out under the duvet and tickled her ribs. "I don't think what we've done this evening is exactly stereotypical. Do you really want to be with Mr. Average?"

He pulled the duvet up over his own head too and kissed her lightly on the mouth. She tasted sweet, of cassis and cocktails.

"Fair point," she agreed once he'd pulled away. She nestled her head into his chest, her whole body seeming to sigh into him. He stroked her hair.

"This is a great bed, Zac. It feels amazing after four weeks in a bunk-bed."

"I see, so you're with me for my bed?"

"Of course, what else?"

He could hear the cheekiness return to her voice, it made him smile. "How about my wit and charm? Or my obvious talents."

He squeezed her bottom to remind her what they were.

"It certainly wasn't your modesty." She laughed.

"Who needs modesty? There are enough people in the world who'll try and put you down, there's absolutely no need to join in and hand them ammunition."

"How true." She sighed again, her breath tickling his chest. He wanted to know more but knew he had to tread carefully.

"It's strange thinking of myself as a godfather." He mused.

Huh? Where had that come from?

He hadn't been planning to get heavy but it was no good, the urge to share with Flora felt overwhelming.

"I suppose it must be. Is this your first godchild then? And you've no nephews or nieces?"

"Yes, first godchild but not the first of my friends to have kids. With Nick it's different though, he's my best mate, we go way back."

Flora said nothing but her soft warm curves pressed up against him felt comforting and he knew she was listening.

"What do you want to achieve in life, Flora?"

"Erm, I'd like to have fun." She spoke quietly.

There's got to be more…

"Apart from that," he said impatiently. "Everyone wants to do that for a while but then, after that… what do you want to look back on your life and be proud of?"

"I used to love art at school," she replied after a long pause. "I loved designing and creating things. I still make some of my own clothes and design bags. My parents and the school's career advisor persuaded me out of Art College into a more sensible direction. You know, the kind that pays the bills. I did a book-keeping course instead. Exciting, huh?"

There was a flat tone to her voice that spoke volumes.

"But you're here in Verbier for the season? I'd say that's pretty exciting."

"I wanted a change. I needed a challenge." She sighed again, a heartfelt sigh.

Maybe she does get it after all.

"So what would you do if you could? What's your dream job or your fantasy business, say?" His management skills were kicking in, he could feel it. It was exciting to realise he might be able to help Flora, to make a difference to her.

"I'd love to be able to have my own bag range, even get them into the shops somehow. I want to be able to prove them all wrong, that you can make a living from being creative, that it isn't an indulgent waste of my time."

Interesting. Who exactly is it she wants to stick two fingers up to?

"Maybe you can." He decided to shelve the awkward questions for the moment.

"Maybe." Flora yawned loudly.

He could tell she was shattered. He on the other hand was buzzing. He always had trouble switching his mind off for sleep. Biting back the questions he wanted to ask he listened to Flora's breathing pattern change as she fell asleep.

He felt wired, the desire to help Flora tugging relentlessly at his concentration. There was something about her that caught his imagination, she needed someone on her side; he knew it in his guts.

Having a project always made him restless. There was no point trying to sleep. Quietly he reached for his laptop and began to click and read, making notes in a separate Word file.

Time to do some research.

His BlackBerry buzzed nearby. He reached over and grabbed it before it could wake Flora and saw the text was from Nick.

'Still up?'

He slipped out of bed and pulled his jeans on, making his way to the kitchen, where he wouldn't disturb Flora. Then he scrolled through his contacts and hit the button to call Nick.

"Hi mate." Zac grabbed some juice from the fridge. "Congratulations."

"Thanks, it's bloody amazing, really it blows your mind. I held my son in my arms tonight, can you believe it?"

"I know, pretty unbelievable. You – a father!"

Nick seemed to miss the joke, which wasn't like him. Already, Nick had taken a step away from their relationship, even further than when he'd married. Sure, Zac knew how it went, how relationships drifted. He'd just hoped it wouldn't happen to them.

When you didn't have a supportive family, your friends meant that much more to you.

"It's the best feeling ever." Nick's voice bubbled over with enthusiasm, carried away on a tide of euphoria. "You really ought to do it mate."

"Whoa, I haven't done the first step yet."

"Exactly! You've got some catching up to do. What are you waiting for?"

Zac frowned at that. Sure, they'd always been competitive but settling down and starting a family was hardly something you could compete over. After all, his own parents had married young. Much good it had done them.

"You'll end up a lonely old bachelor, mate." Nick added.

"Thanks for that," Zac replied dryly, raising his eyes to the ceiling. "Enough about me. Tell me about that godson of mine…"

When Flora woke it took her a while to work out where she was. She'd expected to wake up in a bunk-bed but instead woke cradled by the most comfortable mattress she'd ever lain on, blinking up at a high vaulted ceiling. Light streamed through the windows stretching up to the apex of the roof. She could see the snow capped Alps from where she lay, vividly contrasted by the brightest of blue skies.

She had so much more space than back in the dorm room. She could stretch out her limbs any way she wanted in the super king bed. It was quite a change.

As was the super-fit guy sitting up in bed by her side. He was working on his laptop looking as fresh as the pristine snow that'd fallen during the night.

"Morning." He smiled. "Sleep well?"

"Very well thanks," she replied, wondering how she was going to manage the naked dash to the bathroom. Where in the heck were her clothes?

"I guess it must be nice not having to get up early to make loads of breakfasts for Scott's paying guests?" He asked. "I have coffee and croissants if you're hungry."

"Sounds good." She smiled awkwardly, wondering how he could be so unfazed by this.

Lots of practice Flora. Get used to it. This is what it's like being back in the dating world – coping with the morning after…

As embarrassing as being naked under the duvet was she was more worried about last night. Had her inexperience been really obvious? Had she made a twat of herself?

It wasn't the kind of subject you could casually bring up over coffee and croissants though, was it?

"I've got a spare dressing gown in the en suite if you like? I'll go and get breakfast and you can use the bathroom."

With relief she streaked to the bathroom once he'd left the room, touched he'd understood her embarrassment. Once the door was locked she let out a sigh of relief. Then she looked in the mirror and relief turned to horror as she noticed the smudged make-up beneath her eyes.

She did not look good.

What am I supposed to do now?

Didn't people vanish after one-night stands? Was this even a one-night stand?

Help!

She squeezed her eyes tightly shut feeling like a small goldfish plunged into a very large ocean. Perhaps she should eat breakfast but then get quickly out before she outstayed her welcome? Was that the polite thing to do?

Sex with Zac had been incredible. Nerve endings she hadn't even known she possessed tingled at the memory of last night.

I've exorcised Tom's ghost.

Mostly.

She hoped Zac wouldn't talk about Scott and Holly's wedding too much. It wasn't his fault, he didn't know today should've been her wedding day and it was hardly a first date topic of conversation. Pain cramped in her stomach and she ignored it. Stress cramps had become a frequent feature of the past six months.

Flora washed her face quickly and put the white waffle robe on. At least a light tan from the winter sun meant her skin didn't look too terrible without make-up. She needed to track her handbag down so she could brush her hair though. She ran her fingers through the tangles, trying to tame her blonde locks into some semblance of style.

I did the right thing by walking out. I had no choice.

She tried to stifle the hurt that accompanied the thought. Tom's family hated her guts and she felt the loss of them every day. They'd been one of the reasons she'd put up with Tom for as long as she had. They were practically her surrogate family given that her own parents had upped and moved to Thailand as soon as she turned eighteen, leaving her rootless and alone.

A fresh wave of fear washed over her as she padded barefoot out of the en suite, submerging her in fear of the future and fear of having to be one hundred per cent responsible for herself with no back up plan and no parents to run home to if it all went wrong.

Get over yourself and grow up Flora! Other people cope.

This option was a hell of a lot better than marrying a man who'd been making her miserable. Did she really want to be still living in a minefield, not knowing which step might trigger an explosion? She liked being with Tash, Sophie and Amelia – they reminded her how much she missed the old friends Tom had gradually squeezed out of their life together. How could she have let that happen? It hadn't seemed to matter too much when she was so close to his sister Cathy.

That would be the same Cathy who wasn't even speaking to her now.

Flora climbed back into the bed. It was a truly gorgeous bed, so much nicer than her creaking bunk-bed back at Chalet Repos.

Zac came into the room, carrying a tray with fresh croissants and a cafetière of coffee. She didn't like to say she was strictly a tea girl.

I'm certainly never being a 'cocktail girl' again…

Her cheeks burned with embarrassment when she thought about what they'd done last night. Those Mojitos had a lot to answer for.

You did it because you wanted to, the drinks didn't make you do it.

She glanced at the muscles still visible beneath Zac's T-shirt. He was gorgeous and seemed lovely. And the connection between them felt pretty… incredible.

Incredibly scary. I don't think I'm ready for this.

"I look a right state." Flora grimaced and pulled the duvet up to her chin. "I'm not sure where I left my bag last night."

"You look lovely, trust me." Zac smiled, putting the tray down on the bedside table. "I put your bag in here with your clothes."

He opened a small cupboard underneath and brought out her evening bag, scrutinising the beadwork closely. "This is really good. I'm guessing you made this, right?"

"Yes," she said, feeling a little shy. "It's one of mine."

"You should definitely do something with this. You're wasted in book-keeping and you can't be a seasonaire forever you know?"

I do know!

Her hand tightened around the croissant she was holding. "Well, yes, obviously I know that."

Emotion bubbled up inside her, she couldn't identify it but it felt dangerous, as though if she didn't control it something catastrophic might happen.

"I did some research for you last night." Zac didn't seem to be picking up her mood. He produced a sheaf of papers.

"Did you sleep at all last night?" She looked incredulously at the paperwork. Instinctively she wanted to withdraw, to pull back into her shell and hide from the world. She didn't want to connect, to share, to expose herself for scrutiny. Her dreams were just that – hers.

And she'd had enough of being told what to do for a lifetime.

"I don't sleep much, only four or five hours a night and when I'm up I like to work, to do something productive, you know?" Zac enthused, spreading the papers out on the bed.

"Right." Flora absently shredded her croissant, her appetite fading. All of a sudden she wanted to be on her own. "It's very kind of you but I don't need your… help."

The bubbling, churning emotion surged inside her. The rapidly rising tide of emotion made her jittery, scared she wouldn't be able to control it. The smile on her face was frozen into place, her cheeks aching. If she left now would that be rude?

Today of all days she needed to be alone. She was an emotional liability – guilt, fear, anger and loss cannoning around inside her, looking for an external target to strike out at. She couldn't unleash the tsunami on Zac, it wouldn't be fair of her.

"I don't mind helping, it's no trouble." Zac didn't seem to be getting the hint, he was too taken up with whatever plan he'd formulated. "I think you need to start small and sell through eBay and etsy.com. Maybe set up an online shop once you've got enough stock. Here are some guides explaining everything you need to know and the taxation implications depending on which country you decide to base yourself in."

Flora slipped out of bed. "That's great Zac, thanks. Look I'm really sorry but I'm afraid I've got to go. I've just remembered I promised to do something for Holly."

"I thought you had some time off?"

"It's, er wedding related stuff," Flora bluffed. "I'll go and get changed and you know… go…"

Really? That's the best you can come up with Flora? Brain, please engage my tongue because you're both doing a crap job!

But the panic was rising inside her.

"Do you want to hang out later? I could teach you to snowboard?"

Flora shuddered inwardly. Accept help in another field in which she was inexperienced and he knew everything? No thanks. Absolutely no way.

If she saw Zac again it had to be on an equal footing. This was freaking her out too much.

"Um, maybe," she replied. "I'll get my phone and we can… trade numbers?"

Zac caught her eye and in a sudden flash she remembered what it had been like having him inside her. She looked away, down at the floor and fled to the en suite to get dressed as quickly as possible.

Once dressed again, finally managing the zip on her dress without asking Zac for help, she bumped into him in the hallway.

"Hey, you forgot these." He handed her the papers, now fastened together with treasury tags.

"Oh, thanks," Flora flushed again, feeling the heat creeping up her neck, her body reacting to their close proximity. How did you say goodbye in these situations? A peck on the cheek? An awkward 'bye then?'

Zac solved the question for her by leaning in to kiss her. Desire responded inside her but she was determined to ignore it this time. She had to be alone. She needed time to think. This was how Tom had worked, confusing her with kisses and kindnesses until she almost doubted her recollections of his other behaviour.

Zac isn't Tom.

She knew that was true, but still… making her feelings subject to logic and reason wasn't something she'd mastered yet.

"I need to go." She headed to the front door, ignoring the spasm of longing surging deep inside her.

"Later?" He quirked an eyebrow, intense blue eyes searching her face as though hoping to read subtitles explaining what was happening between them.

"Perhaps." She smiled and half raised her right arm in an awkward wave. "I'll, er, text you."

"Are you going to be alright walking back?" He eyed her knee-high boots dubiously.

"I'll be fine, it looks like they've cleared the pavements of ice." She smiled and edged away, trying not to meet his eye. "Bye then."

It was a relief to finally stop smiling once she was out of his sight. When she'd been putting Zac's number into her phone she'd noticed a new email alert from Cathy and wanted some privacy to read it. Tom's sister hadn't contacted her in months.

Maybe it's a peace offering at last?

She was glad her coat covered up what was obviously an evening dress. Other seasonaires might call this the 'walk of pride,' but to Flora it felt like a walk of shame.

Today was supposed to be my wedding day. I would've been wearing my wedding dress…

But how could she have married Tom? She stepped carefully over a pile of snow not yet cleared and made herself think about Zac instead.

He had only been trying to help.

You were rude.

But whatever happened next in her life had to be her decision, her plan, her actions…

One hundred per cent independence might be lonely but it was the only way to go. She had to stick to it, not be swayed by the first man to show an interest in her. A non-sexual interest as well as fancying her, that was. Plenty of men had tried to induce her to join in with the bed hopping, or some cringey 'fondle-her-in-a-gondola.' She hated that phrase and she'd also refused invitations to the 'nearly naked' Sunday evening bar sessions – just a blatant excuse for all the cocky exhibitionists in Verbier to take their clothes off.

At least she only stripped in private!

Neither did she sneak over the fence to get into the Hotel Royale's Jacuzzi – the place to be in the evening if you fancied getting it on with other like-minded seasonaires.

Somehow she didn't think last night had changed all that for her. She was never going to be *that* girl. Intimacy was hard enough without the risk that among all those strangers she might accidentally pick someone like Tom.

Flora rubbed her hands together to keep them warm. The sky was blue but the sun hadn't reached this part of town yet. It would be lovely up on the slopes today, maybe she should hit the pistes instead of moping. It would take her mind off everything. Since when had feeling sorry for yourself ever solved anything?

She wished she hadn't let her herself think about Tom last night. Thinking about *that night*, the most awful of her entire life, was like a car crash – you wanted to look away but found yourself staring over the crash barriers nonetheless. She could understand the reasons why Tom had acted as he did but she'd never be able to excuse him. His father's heart attack and convalescence had put pressure on Tom, leaving him to run the business.

She'd sympathised until he'd increasingly taken his frustrations out on her. The first time he'd crossed the line he'd lost his temper and shoved her against a wall during a row. He'd convinced her afterwards it was an accident. She'd believed him because she wanted to.

She'd been stupid.

For months she'd been thinking about leaving but every time she came close he seemed to sense it and did something so lovely and caring she began to seriously doubt her own judgement. It'd seemed selfish to leave him when he was under so much pressure.

And his family, well she hadn't wanted to leave them either. She'd known cancelling the wedding would break his mother's heart at a time when she was worried sick about her husband. Leaving felt cruel and selfish.

But then Tom had punched her and her world had tilted on its axis.

CHAPTER FOUR

"Hi there, dirty stop-out!" Tash was slipping into her ski boots outside Chalet Repos, her skis propped up against a wall. "Didn't expect to see you back so soon. Why aren't you still holed up with the stud from last night?"

Flora shrugged, kicking at a bit of ice at the side of the path.

"Like that is it? Fancy joining us?" Tash asked, bending over to snap the boots into place. "We're all doing the run over to Italy, to Courmayeur for lunch." It sounded like the perfect distraction. "Sounds like a plan. Just give me a chance to get changed."

Fresh air and sunshine had to help, surely?

"You've got at least ten minutes I reckon. The others are on a go-slow after last night. There are some sore heads in there. And baby Lexie woke everyone up at five am too. Still, it's such a great forecast and the fresh air should blow the cobwebs and bad tempers away."

Flora raced to the dorm room, getting changed as quickly as she could in the small space considering Amelia and Sophie were also getting dressed. She did her best to deflect their questions about Zac. The email from Cathy was burning a hole in her pocket but there was no time to act on it. Truth be told she was scared to open it. As long as she didn't read it she could hope it might be good news, an olive branch email.

Finally, while they were standing in the snow, waiting for the telecabine, she decided she had to open the email. She took her phone out of the pocket of her ski jacket and opened the email. Almost immediately she wished she hadn't.

She stared at the screen, frozen to the spot even though the queue had moved on, barely noticing the mutterings of the people behind her.

"Hey, earth to Flora. What's up?" Tash pulled on her elbow, propelling her forward on her skis. Flora was taken by surprise and almost fell over backwards into a snowdrift, only just managing to right herself in time.

"I've changed my mind. I just want to sit back in one of the deckchairs at the canteen and get some sun. I don't feel up to a big day out and I've got some emails to do."

She clutched her phone tightly, waving it as though to make her point and feeling a tad unhinged. How could she even start to process this latest assault?

"Are you sure?" Tash seemed distracted, looking ahead at the rest of the gang. She clearly wanted to go, not act as a nursemaid to Flora. It would be selfish to ask her to stay.

"Go on. I'll be fine." Flora forced a smile and waved Tash off.

Liar.

She snapped out of her skis and put them into a rack, her hands shaking. Then she joined the other sunbathers and skiers taking a break, sinking down onto a bright red canteen deckchair. She shaded the screen of her phone from the sunshine so she could re-read the email. There was no 'dear' or even a 'Hi' at the start of the email. Just the plain stark facts with lashings of screaming subtext.

"Dad died of a heart attack yesterday morning. The doctors said that stress was a major contributor. I hope you think the price you paid to go off and 'find yourself' was worth it."

The unfairness of it was a vicious kick to the kidneys.

Tears rolled down behind Flora's sunglasses and onto her cheeks.

She tried to cry silently so she wouldn't draw attention to herself.

She'd been fond of Bob, he'd been so much more fatherly than her own dad and a kind boss to work for, however much she'd found the work boring. It'd been Bob who'd shown her how to change the oil in her car and how to use a power drill to put up pictures.

My fault. My fault. My fault…

She almost choked on her sobs, the breath catching in her chest, her body flooded with grief as the tears streamed down her cheeks. It didn't seem to matter she hadn't had a choice. Everyone hated her. Tom's mum would blame her too. Margaret had already railed at her for 'breaking my poor Tom's heart.'

She'd never been able to tell them about Tom punching her. Whether it was from irrational shame and shock or genuine pity and desire to prevent further grief she didn't know. It was probably a mixture of all of the above. All she knew for sure was that when she tried to talk about it the words just wouldn't come.

And all she'd cared about at the time was getting away. She'd been certain they would always back Tom over her.

Looks like I was right…

Of course they had. They'd never really been *her* family.

She couldn't summon up enough embarrassment to check the tears running down her cheeks. Her fighting spirit had been crushed and at that moment she felt more lost than she ever had. She thought she'd bottomed out months ago. It went to show you could never let your guard down. The next shock or slap in the face might be just around the corner.

"Hey Flora." She heard Zac's voice before she saw him, her vision too blurred with tears. He touched her lightly on the arm. "I was about to get a coffee and sit in the sun. I see you've had the same idea."

Then he fell quiet, she guessed he'd seen the tears escaping from beneath her sunglasses.

"What's wrong?" He frowned at her. "Is this about last night?"

"No… oo," she choked out an answer through her sobs.

He crouched down next to her and with embarrassment she realised she couldn't control her sobs. The tears kept pouring out.

The dam had well and truly burst and she couldn't do a thing about it.

"I'm, s... s... sorry." She looked into his face, the compassion she saw there only made her feel even worse.

Great way to make an impression. So much for playing it cool.

"Hey." Zac pulled her sunglasses off and when he saw her face he sank down onto his knees in the snow, pulling her closely to his chest.

She let him hold her, feeling limper than a rag doll. All the breath had been knocked out of her by the email, the bereavement, the blame…

I should be able to deal with this. I will deal with it. But right now, right this second, I can't.

"What's up?" He pulled back a little to examine her face.

She stared wordlessly at him, aware of the other canteen clientele staring at them but too distraught to pull herself together.

Great! I haven't cried for months and I choose here and now to have a mini meltdown?

Where on earth did she start?

"It's complicated." She sniffed, grimacing in acknowledgement of the cliché but more concerned about whether she could find a tissue for her runny nose in any of her pockets. Looking like crap in front of Zac was clearly *de rigeur*.

"I've got time for complicated, I'm not going anywhere," he replied, his eyes serious, searching her face as though looking for clues of how he could solve her.

He likes me…

The thought flashed into her mind, jolting her and making her senses tingle. The realisation sent a ray of light into her murky thoughts. With everyone in her old life either hating her like Cathy or indifferent like her parents, having someone like Zac actively seeking her out felt like a life raft on this ocean of turbulent emotions.

"Can we go back to your chalet?" The words tumbled out of her mouth before she'd had time to talk herself out of it. She needed to feel wanted and affirmed. She needed Zac to distract her if today wasn't going to be a total disaster. She should never have run away this morning.

And she had a pretty good idea how he might be able to do it.

"Okay. Do you need to put your skis in a locker? I can take them for you if you like?"

"Thank you." Flora was profoundly grateful; relieved he cared enough to take her on with her mess, runny nose and all. Because, she had to face it – yesterday she'd been trying, pretty unsuccessfully to channel her inner sex kitten but today her inner neurotic was running the show. And why exactly had she over reacted and fled earlier?

I really need to get my head together.

"I'm so sorry," Flora apologised when Zac returned, feeling wretched.

"There's nothing to be sorry for. Something's clearly wrong and you don't need to be ashamed of your reaction. Bottling it all up is what messes with your head."

"Oh. Are you talking from experience?" She looked up at him. They'd discarded their ski gloves and he laced his fingers through hers.

"Yes, I'm talking from experience," Zac replied shortly. She waited but he said nothing more.

Clearly he was of the 'strong and silent' mould. Well that worked for her.

Electricity crackled between them again and the familiar gut churning anticipation mingled with unease. She wasn't sure which element was the most powerful.

She wondered what lay behind Zac's comment. He seemed so sorted, as though he had everything worked out and might be able to help her figure it out too.

Yet everything inside her screamed at her to keep him at arm's length. She couldn't cope with anything heavy right now. Or ever, in fact…

Independence remember?

Sod independence for the next few hours. She wanted company. Needed to experience her body fused with another's, to feel connected and affirmed.

To feel alive.

Once in the chalet she stripped off her jacket and boots, walking in her socks straight to the bedroom. She didn't want time to change her mind.

Wordlessly she tugged at fastenings and zips.

Zac watched her, hesitating before stripping, his expression impassive but his eyes dark with desire. "Are you sure? Don't you need to talk first?"

"No." She looked at him, pleadingly. "I need this first. Please?"

God, this is the second time I've begged him for sex. So classy!

But she didn't feel humiliated, this felt okay, natural almost.

"Come here then." He beckoned her over and she went, willing, if only for a few hours, to let him take control. Maybe he'd do a better job of it than her.

Undoubtedly.

He tugged her long-sleeved T-shirt over her head and pulled her into his arms. Then he kissed her, trailing his lips down to her neck and chest, sucking and teasing at her nipples through the lacy fabric of her bra. They stiffened in response, making her desperate to be pressed against him, skin against skin.

Her hands slid over his chest, caressing his already familiar flesh. His muscles felt solid and reassuring. She grinned at him as he undid her bra clasp and soon they were pulling at clothes, throwing off every vestige of clothing.

They explored each other, running hands over curves and muscle, fingers entangled in hair, pulling and tugging closer, groaning with desire.

When Zac slid a hand up to caress her between her legs, dipping two fingers inside her, she was already dripping wet. He teased her with his thumb and she groaned, arching towards him and sighing with pleasure when he clasped one of her breasts. It felt deliciously carnal and liberating to ignore all her anxieties and reservations. Like dancing naked on a lawn, ignoring a sign telling her to 'keep off the grass.'

Just for a few hours.

Their breathing was laboured and ragged, their pupils dilated and their focus entirely on each other's body.

She reached down to caress his erection and he jerked to her touch.

"Please," she half begged, half groaned. "I need..."

What do I need?

She wasn't sure but all her instincts lead her to Zac, vaulting the doubts and reservations that would no doubt launch a counter attack later. But what the hell? They weren't in control now.

Make me forget.

He backed her towards the edge of the bed and firmly pushed her down, spreading her legs with the palms of his hands and pulling her wide open in front of him. The daylight made it impossible to hide. She didn't care. She wanted it. Wanted him. Wanted to blot out the pain.

She closed her eyes, the darkness intensifying the sensation of Zac's lips on her thighs. Moaning softly she lay back on the bed, spreading her arms out and opening herself, uncurling and blossoming to the touch of his tongue.

As the kisses trailed higher up her thighs she tensed a little but tried to override her fear, making no move to stop him. After a pause he continued to kiss higher up, licking and caressing her sex, tongue teasing.

She couldn't look at him, couldn't meet the connection she experienced whenever their eyes locked. She focused instead on the sweet pleasure throbbing between her legs, piercing her and splitting her in two as she bucked beneath his tongue and climaxed.

She kept her eyes shut when she heard the rip of a foil packet and felt his erection brush her thigh.

"Look at me." Zac's words were quiet but insistent.

Reluctantly she opened her eyes, her gaze meeting his and then dropping to where he had positioned himself at her sex. It turned her on to see him erect and clearly desiring her.

"You're okay Flora, you're okay." He whispered and the tight vice around her heart loosened its grip. Tension and air released from her lungs in a deep sigh. She raised her legs to hook them around his hips, pulling him into her, gasping when he entered her hard and deep.

She met every thrust with passion, eyes wide open, feeling freer with each stroke, the rhythm producing a steady hum in her clit and the deep angle creating sensations she'd never felt before.

Is this my G-spot waking up?

Previously undiscovered nerve endings tingled and throbbed inside her, caressed and massaged with every thrust.

Zac put a hand under her bottom and squeezed. He held her so firmly she had no option but to grip him even harder.

Then she came for a second time but this was a longer ride, her whole body taken over by the tide of endorphins sweeping away her sadness as he tensed and cried out, reaching his climax at the same time as she came.

Flora was a puzzle. It was as though Zac had to look at her out of the corner of his eye because if he faced her head-on then the real, genuine girl he was coming to like very much would vanish. She seemed so easily spooked. Look at her awkward exit this morning.

On the one hand it was frustrating.

On the other it was captivating.

She had his interest. It'd been re-kindled when he'd seen her sitting on her own at the mountain canteen, sitting so rigidly still he'd known something was wrong.

He hadn't been able to bear the bleak look in her eyes when he'd taken her sunglasses off. Her earlier irritation at his efforts to help her, however much she'd tried to hide it, had rubbed at him like a badly fitting ski boot. But one look at Flora's tear sodden face and something had tugged deep inside him, a primal urge to draw her to him and try to take care of her, if she'd let him.

The urge to fix and help was such a strong one he'd never been able to resist it – from injured birds and stray dogs as a child to broken women. This felt like something more than his usual cursed inability to ever let anything go. It was a deep connection that blew him away whenever Flora allowed herself to look into his eyes, whenever she didn't shy away from him like a wild horse evading a lasso.

Flora climbed back into his bed, drawing the duvet up over her body, hiding again, her urgency seemingly depleted. He slid in next to her, pulling her into his arms, cuddling her back. He wondered if she'd be more likely to talk to him if she couldn't see his face.

Obviously she was ashamed of something but he really didn't see what she could've done that would be so terrible.

"You need to talk about it," he said, lazily stroking her arm.

"I just found out someone I cared about has passed away. He died of a heart attack and it was a bit of a shock."

"I'm sorry to hear that," Zac murmured quietly. "Did you know him well?"

"Yes, he was my ex's dad and my old boss. And, well, there's something else – it was supposed to be my wedding day today." Flora sighed as she snuggled back against him.

"Oh?"

Whatever I was imagining I wasn't expecting that.

"Yep. But I couldn't do it, he was… wrong for me."

Zac stayed silent but continued to stroke, to soothe, to encourage her words to flow with the tips of his fingers. Teasing her words from her as he'd teased her body earlier.

"I couldn't cope with his mood swings and he was controlling, really controlling, you know?"

"I think I do, yes," Zac sighed, pulling her closer, the stirrings of anger bubbling deep inside him. The dormant volcano always rumbled, the lava of anger churning in his belly, whenever something happened to remind him of his father.

He'd had a masterclass in the controlling type in his dad. The thought of Flora involved with anyone like his dad made his gut clench.

"Then you did the right thing."

"How can you be so sure?" She twisted round to face him, seemingly ready to engage. "I haven't even told you everything..."

"Do you want to tell me?"

"Not... right now... Sorry."

"That's fine. But can you tell me why you were crying earlier? You said it was meant to be your wedding day. Was it that or... did something happen earlier? Has someone upset you?" She definitely hadn't been this upset earlier when she'd left his chalet. Distant yes, but not distraught.

If anyone's hurt her, I'll...

"The email I got earlier telling me about the heart attack, it came from my ex's sister, we used to be good friends." She bit her lip and her eyes filled with tears again. "The family blame me, they say it was stress..."

He wiped away a tear on her cheek with his thumb.

"Hey." He placed a soft kiss on her trembling lower lip. "You can't take responsibility for someone else's health or their actions. You could hardly marry just to keep the in-laws happy, that's not fair."

"I sort of know that on one level," she admitted, eyes huge and threatening to brim over again. "But he was like family to me. My own parents aren't really the happy family types. Tom's family became my family and they were under a lot of stress. Maybe I should have stayed, helped them. Perhaps I was selfish."

He gently nudged her shoulders to bring her back from the

dark place she'd vanished to.

"No excuses. Don't make excuses for him," he said, exasperated, her story so horribly familiar it prodded and bated the slumbering volcano through the iron bars of his control. "Did he make you miserable? Undermine you? Belittle you?"

Did he hurt you?

She nodded slowly.

Zac took a deep breath. "Were you afraid of him?"

"Yes," she replied, burying her face deep into the pillow.

He wanted to bring back the sassy girl who'd walked up to him in the bar and surprised him with a kiss, the girl who had dreams and a talent that'd been stifled.

His jaw tensed and he closed his eyes for a minute, trying to contain the volcano, trying not to think about the things that would lead to its eruption. He held her, murmuring nonsense and trying to comfort her while hiding his own turmoil. It took all his control to prevent the rigid fear that had crept into his muscles from spreading throughout his body like a crippling virus. He hoped she couldn't feel it.

"It's okay," he whispered.

"I wish it could be," she replied after a pause.

"You're here and you're safe." He said. "And you're not responsible."

She shuddered against him, turning and running her hands over his body, stoking his desire again.

His brain argued that this wasn't wise. She was vulnerable… but it was what she wanted, maybe what she needed. Sex could be healing and life affirming; he knew that.

And right now there wasn't anything else he'd rather been doing. The holiday period yawned out ahead of him, it was ages before the office re-opened and he'd be busy again.

If he was honest with himself he needed this as much as she did. Flora kissed him passionately and then pulled away.

"What were you planning to do today?" She shuffled up the bed and sat up. "I'm sorry, I've ruined your day on the slopes. Were you heading for the Snow Park at La Chaux, isn't that where all the boarders go?"

"It's fine, I've been quite happy with the other activities on offer." Zac lightly squeezed her thigh under the duvet. "We could go get some lunch if you're up to it."

"Maybe not the canteen." Flora rolled her eyes. "They must think I'm a nutter."

"Hardly. You won't be the first person to ever cry in public." He shrugged.

"Have you ever cried in public?" She raised an eyebrow.

"Well… no. In fact... I haven't ever cried, not that I can remember." Zac shifted uncomfortably, wishing they could get back to the subject of lunch.

"What, never?" Her eyes widened.

"Erm, no." The uncomfortable sensation stretched its grip into her chest.

I would never give him the satisfaction of knowing he'd got to me.

"Shall we go sit in the sun for lunch? Fancy a Croque Monsieur?"

I never cried because I couldn't.

"Okay." She stared at him as though reading his thoughts.

He looked away, unnerved.

Sitting in the warm winter sunshine Flora titled her head back and let the warmth heal and restore her.

Maybe this could be a short-term fling? If she set an end to it, a 'best before' date, then she could have fun without worrying about getting involved.

Because she needed to be single, had to be much stronger than she felt right now, before she started on a new relationship. But a fling with Zac needn't jeopardise that.

"You look happy." Zac had returned from the bar and put the drinks down on the wooden trestle table of the Chalet-style bar.

The wedding. I'll let myself see Zac until Holly's wedding. After that there'll be no reason to see him again, it will be easier to make a break before it can get too heavy. I'm just dipping my toe in the water, that's all…

"It must be the Zac effect." She grinned. Her body certainly appreciated his way of cheering her up. Every inch of skin had been thoroughly caressed, she was sure she glowed from the attentions he'd lavished on her. "Maybe we should market it?"

"I think I'll stick to the day job." Zac laughed. The darkness she'd seen in his eyes earlier had disappeared.

How can someone never cry?

What was Zac's secret? Everyone had secrets.

Even she had stuff she'd never told a soul, simply could not talk about. She liked that Zac had seen her at her messiest worst and was still here. He hadn't gone running for the mountain peaks. She was sure a lesser guy would have.

"So what is the day job?"

"I'm a management consultant, I work in Geneva, I have a flat there. Do you know Geneva very well?"

"Not really." She shrugged apologetically. "I went straight to the train station when I got off the plane."

"I'll have to show you round. What are you doing for Christmas?"

"I'm tagging on to Holly and Scott's Christmas, they've got lots of guests over for the wedding. It'll be a little awkward I think. Scott's parents are coming and I think I'm going to feel in the way."

"So you're not using the time off to see your parents?"

"No, my parents live in Thailand and they aren't really into Christmas, never have been." She grimaced, thinking about one unhappy childhood Christmas in particular. She'd spent it wishing her family could be like everybody else's – longing for a Christmas tree or stocking fillers at the end of her bed instead of a lecture on the immorality of consumerism and being told to give her Christmas money to charity. She'd only been eight!

If I ever have children I'm going to spoil them rotten.

She blinked hard.

"What about you? Where are your family based?"

"They live just outside Geneva, a little town called Coppet. I've no siblings, I'm an only child."

"Oh, me too! So, you're going to theirs for Christmas day?"

Fleetingly she thought of her own parents and wished she had someone waiting for her for Christmas lunch.

"No," he replied abruptly, his jaw tensing and the darkness she'd seen earlier reappearing to shadow his features.

She reached under the table to stroke his leg, saying nothing. Gratifyingly he relaxed his rigid posture.

"Would you like to hang out for Christmas? I know somewhere I think you'd love. It would be fun to have some company and such a shame not to use your time off to see a bit of Switzerland. What with Scott only employing Brits and catering to the UK market you're not really experiencing Swiss culture."

Fun, yes. Nothing heavy. Hanging out was nice and casual.

"I'd like to do that, thanks." She smiled, relaxing. "Am I allowed to know where we're going?"

"I think I'll keep it as a surprise," he shifted in his chair. "And tickling my leg isn't going to persuade me."

She laughed and withdrew her hand. "Looks like I need to spend some time finding your ticklish spot."

"Or we could play Truth or Dare again."

Truth – I like you. Dare – I dare myself to spend time with you without getting in too deep. Forfeit? Hmm, I'd be very happy to give up my bunk-bed and exchange it for your king size bed.

Very happy indeed.

Hanging out wasn't the same as going out. Everyone knew that. And if she ended it after the wedding it needn't turn into anything serious. She had to believe that because what Zac was offering her was far too tempting to turn down…

CHAPTER FIVE

Flora just about managed not to drool as she followed Zac into the plush entrance of the Mirador Kempinski. Soothing classical music played in the background and a delicious scent of jasmine permeated the air. Uniformed staff beamed at them as though they were the most important people on the planet.

She'd thought he was taking her to some kind of remote log cabin or something authentic, not to a five star spa hotel. She wandered over to the plate glass wall that ran the length of the lobby to look at the view while Zac talked to the staff.

"Wow," she exclaimed, taking in the magnificent view down across Lac Léman to Evian and the French Alps. The mountains sparkled ice white with fresh snowfall, contrasting with the vivid blue of the sky. Down below the lake shimmered and danced in the sunlight, dotted with tiny boats with billowing sails.

It was possibly the best view she'd ever seen in her life.

"I thought you'd like the view here. It's quite something, isn't it?" Zac turned towards her, smiling at her reaction.

"We've upgraded you to the Presidential suite sir." The front of house man handed Zac a form to sign. "If you'd both like to come with me? Don't worry about your bags, Mademoiselle, they will be brought to the room and if you give us your car key we'll make sure it's parked for you."

Flora's eyebrows shot up when she saw the suite. She tried to bite back her reaction – it wasn't cool to act too excitedly, was it? But this was the best hotel room she'd ever seen. It was easily three times the size of the flat she'd shared with Tom back in England. It had its own sitting room and library, not to mention its own dining room, kitchen area with cappuccino machine and three separate terraces to sit out on, all overlooking the jaw-dropping view. The bathroom had a sumptuous Jacuzzi bath set into the middle of the floor and enticing packets of bath salts and expensive lotions.

When they were finally left alone Flora turned to Zac, grinning wildly.

"This is the best Christmas present anyone's ever given me. It's fantastic here, I'm not sure I ever want to leave!"

"Glad you like it. I must admit I wasn't expecting to be upgraded, they must have had a cancellation, or… perhaps they thought my father had made the booking, I didn't leave my first name." Zac gazed pensively out at the view, frowning. "Oh well, we're here, that's what matters."

"Who is your father?" she asked. "Someone important?"

"Sort of – he's known locally at least." Zac turned to her and pulled her into a hug. "And my parents dine at Le Patio fairly often but anyway, I don't want to talk about them. It's nice to spend Christmas with someone… special."

"Oh, I'm special am I?" She nudged him playfully and snuggled into his chest, trying hard not to think about what would happen when this was over. She just had to try to hold back emotionally. Just? Huh, because that was going to be easy, wasn't it?

"Oh yes." Zac pulled her over closer to him, his hands on the small of her back. "Don't you know you're special?"

Flora thought hard. Her parents had never been particularly demonstrative or generous with their praise. She'd always been left feeling distinctly lacking, never quite able to measure up to their high standards. Tom had sometimes made her feel special but then he'd also made her feel as worthless as it was possible to feel too.

"Well… I suppose," she lied. She wanted to believe she could be special, but…

How special can this relationship be if I've already set a 'best-before' date on it?

It wasn't meant to mean anything. They were hanging out for the holidays, both at a loose end, keen to enjoy each other's company.

But it's going to be sad when Christmas is over and we go our separate ways…

The rogue thought was accompanied by a swell of longing so powerful it scared her. To avoid having to examine where it'd come from and what it meant she leant up on tiptoe to kiss Zac, closing her eyes to the connection she found in him.

What sort of game were they playing here? What had started out as Truth or Dare had become a whole lot more serious. Did they even know the rules? Perhaps they were making them up as they went along as they had with the Truth or Dare.

Truth – I really, really like you. Dare – I don't dare let this take over. Forfeit – I'm afraid of losing my independence. More than that I'm afraid of losing myself again…

But the thoughts faded away as they kissed, kissed passionately and touched each other as though they were racing time. Soon all she could think about was feeling his skin against hers and wanting him to come inside her again.

The best kind of therapy – the euphoric sex haze that makes everything feel better.

"You do know you're not to blame, don't you?" Zac asked Flora, idly stroking her back; she had such beautifully soft skin. It surprised him how quickly he'd come to care for Flora. He wanted to spoil her, protect her and make her smile. She had a lovely, sexy smile that made her eyes sparkle.

Christmas Eve had been magical with drinks in the Piano bar and a gourmet meal at Le Trianon. He wanted to make her Christmas Day even better. She needed cheering up and as far as he could tell she really didn't deserve the grief she was getting from back home.

He wanted to help her forget.

"Yes… I think I do… now, that is. See what found its way into my timeline yesterday." She handed him her mobile phone, grimacing.

Zac scrolled down to the Facebook link and clicked it, seeing Flora's name mentioned. It linked to a local newspaper article in England.

'**Tragedy Strikes Local Community**' – Earlier this year we reported the heart attack of the chairman of the Parish Council, Mr Paxton, at a community fundraising gathering. Further tragedy struck the Paxton household when his son Tom was jilted at the altar. The runaway bride left the family with mounting bills for a lavish wedding. With regret we report that on hearing the news Mr Paxton went on to have a second heart attack from which he failed to recover. The family blame the cancellation of the wedding and his son's distress for putting Mr Paxton under stress. Mrs. Paxton said…'

Zac stopped reading and raised his eyes to meet Flora's. "You know this is a load of crap don't you?"

She met his eye. "Until I read that article I couldn't shake the guilt but that, that… so-called newspaper gets all its facts wrong. I didn't leave them in any debt; we had wedding insurance and I hardly left Tom at the altar. They got the order of events completely wrong and… I'm bloody angry. It's woken me up to how unfair this is. I think the Paxton's have friends at the local newspaper, it's a deliberate smear and I refuse to let it get to me."

"You could complain? Try to get Facebook to take the link down, or make an official press complaint in England?"

"I don't want to do anything." She shook her head. "If I do I'll get sucked in and I want to leave it all behind me."

He supposed he could understand that point of view. After all hadn't that been the way he always dealt with problems?

"Did you never talk to his family about why you were leaving?"

he asked.

"I tried to." She sighed, shaking her head. "His sister and I were close but I… couldn't tell them how he made me feel. I tried but his sister accused me of making stuff up to make myself look better."

"How bad was it Flora?" He stroked her arms, soothing and cajoling her, the action feeling instinctive.

Somehow he knew it had been *bad.*

He wasn't sure how he knew it. But he knew.

And he wanted to knock the living daylights out of Flora's ex, anger swelling up on her behalf, so strongly that the muscles in his hands tensed and his body felt rigid.

"Pretty bad," she whispered, eyes wide, imploring him to understand. Or did she just want him to shut up and stop asking questions?

He pulled her closer towards him and she pressed her head against his chest, eyes screwed shut.

"It's hard to talk about, you know?"

"I know," he replied, stroking the length of her back. "But it's over now. And you did the right thing. You had to leave. No one should have to put up with bullying of any kind."

His mouth tightened as he thought of his mother and her refusal of all his offers of help.

Her refusal to leave.

It baffled him. Maybe Flora would be able to explain to him why his mum still put up with his dad because he as sure as hell couldn't fathom it!

Can I tell Flora?

He didn't share his family stuff with anyone. It had certainly never occurred to him to share it with the girls he dated. Nick knew things weren't right at home but they never talked about it. It simply wasn't their way of doing things…

He was about to say something when Flora turned her face up to his and kissed him, the kiss was long and deep and passionate, stirring him on every level. Opening Pandora's box could wait until another day.

Who wanted to talk about sad stuff when you could be enjoying life and living it to the full?

Focusing on the positives, that's what I need to do.

And what Flora was doing with her hands most definitely fell into the enjoying life category. She trailed kisses down his chest and surprised him by kneeling down and taking him in her mouth, eyes looking up, wide and focused on him.

She didn't break eye contact when he stared back. The intensity of the connection increased the pleasure for him. It was amazingly, mind-blowingly intimate and he came quickly, unable to hold back or delay his release.

He wanted to repay her, to make her forget about crappy guys who got off on making women feel small. He manoeuvred her back towards the bed, hands running over her body, stroking her curves, and kissing her.

"Let me give you a Christmas present." He grinned.

And then his phone rang.

Some nagging sixth sense told him he couldn't ignore this call. It was Christmas Day. He could never ignore his phone without wondering if his mum was okay.

"I'm sorry," He shot an agonised look at Flora. "It could be important."

He grabbed his phone, the caller ID on the screen told him his fears were well grounded. He answered the call.

All he could hear was his mother sobbing, over and over.

It broke his heart.

"Mum, are you okay?" It was a bloody stupid question but all his brain could come up with at the moment.

There was some more sobbing. And then the line went dead.

He stared at the phone in his hand, dread trickling down his spine. He was dimly aware of Flora's gaze on him and turned back towards her. She sat naked on the edge of the bed, eyes brimming with concern. He liked that she didn't feel the need to hide her gorgeous body under the duvet anymore.

She'll understand. Even if you don't tell her everything she'll understand. Flora's that kind of girl.

"Problem?" she asked.

"Yes." He squeezed his eyes shut for a moment, trying to summon the control he needed to do this. "I have to go."

"Would you like me to come with you?" Flora suggested tentatively.

He considered. An outsider would most likely make his dad snap back into jovial host mode, all traces of his aggression hidden by the smooth veneer of charm and social graces. Zac had seen the transformation more times than he could remember when family friends and colleagues visited them at home.

"Are you sure you don't mind?" He grimaced. "I'm sorry, I'd planned to take you to the Piano Bar for cocktails again later on and we're going to miss our booking for Christmas lunch... This isn't what you signed up for."

"I signed something?" She smiled. "Hey, the hotel's lovely but I'm here to hang out with you."

"Thanks." He grabbed his clothes. "Let's get going then."

He had a feeling this might be a very bad idea but he hoped he'd be proven wrong…

Flora's stomach was churning. She could tell from Zac's stiff jaw and the way he gripped the steering wheel that something was seriously wrong. That he'd fallen out with his parents was obvious given they were practically around the corner and yet he'd chosen not to visit them for Christmas. But it was also clear that he still cared about his mother at least.

If her experiences had taught her anything it was not to judge. You never had all the facts about someone else's situation. She'd experienced enough condemnation to have that lesson drummed into her.

"Am I allowed to ask what's wrong?" She reached across from

where she sat in the passenger seat of his jeep and tentatively laid a hand on his thigh.

"My mum needs some help," he muttered, gaze focused on the road, eyes dark and full of dark intensity.

Help with what? Chopping carrots? Carving the turkey? Do they even have turkey at Christmas here? Well I suppose they might given she's English.

But of course it wasn't going to be anything that trivial. Zac had always seemed so utterly in control but now she could practically see the turbulent emotions warring beneath his calm exterior. His knuckles were virtually white where they gripped the steering wheel.

Every so often he glanced over at her, eyes thoughtful and lips slightly parted as though he was about to speak. But he always seemed to think better of it.

She liked Coppet, it was a pretty little village on the outskirts of Geneva, on the shore of Lac Léman, complete with chateau. Once they'd driven through the main village they took a turning off the road and onto a grand gravel driveway, the house not even in sight from the wrought iron gates. When they eventually did see the house Flora had to admit she was impressed. It was built in the style of a typical French mansion and had pretty green shutters with a snowy white clematis trailing up the creamy brick walls. The grounds were immaculately kept with barely a leaf out of place. To the side of the house Flora's gaze fell on the stretch of private lakeshore and the boathouse. She glanced at Zac, wondering if she should make small talk about the house, tell him how much she liked it.

Maybe not.

He hesitated on the doorstep, face pale and preoccupied. Then he raised his hand and rang the bell. They stood in awkward silence for a few minutes.

"Are you sure they're in?" Flora bit her lip, feeling increasingly uncomfortable, like she was trespassing or something.

Zac pulled a key out of his pocket but hesitated again before putting it into the keyhole. He glanced at Flora, gave her a tight smile that she took to be a 'thanks for this' and then swung the door open.

She could hear the raised voices before they had taken many steps into the elegant hallway. They were speaking French but there was something about the male voice that made her tense, the hectoring tone familiar. Her stomach twisted violently and she placed a hand against the cool stone wall. Zac didn't seem to notice as he strode forward to the source of the row.

The voice could easily have been Tom's in thirty years time. And the woman's voice, low and pleading, sent a chill down her spine.

I used to plead like that. Much good it did me.

Flora hesitated where she stood, one hand on the cool stone and the other on her stomach. Should she go with Zac, or…

A scream cut through her thoughts and Zac strode off ahead of her.

Flora followed tentatively, wondering if she should help but half wanting to go back to the car and shut herself in. She felt physically sick, as though her defences were crashing down around her and her body was letting her down.

She entered a large drawing room in time to see a man in his sixties, presumably Zac's father, with his hands around a slender woman's neck.

Zac raced forward and yanked his father away, then pushed him so hard the man staggered and fell backwards into a chair. The woman ran to the fallen man's aid, her eyes flashing accusation at Zac.

She then stood behind her husband as though literally hiding behind him. Flora froze in the doorway, hoping if she stayed still enough then maybe no one would see her.

"How could you Zac?" The woman's English accent sounded clipped and slightly upper class, Flora had to admire her swift recovery of composure. Her clothes were smart, probably designer.

Most people wouldn't be able to tell anything from looking at her now, her face a mask.

But Flora knew. She knew from one look in the woman's eyes… and she would have known even if she hadn't seen the Zac's dad trying to strangle her. This was classic avoidance.

And she knew it because she'd been there herself.

"I was defending you mum. We should call the police." Zac raised his arms in the air, hurt so vivid in his eyes that for a second she imagined she could see the boy he'd once been. "What is it going to take for you to realise he can't treat you like this? Exactly how far does he have to go?"

"He doesn't mean any harm," his mother whispered, eyes cast down to the hands clasping the chair back in front of her.

Zac snorted.

His father merely sat, glaring at Zac as though his son had climbed out from under a rock and he was contemplating ways of exterminating him.

Anger bubbled inside Flora, causing emotions she'd successfully buried to rise to the surface.

"Why are you here anyway Zac?" His mother asked coldly. "You know we always go to the country club on Christmas Day."

"You rang me." Zac shot an angry look at his father, as though daring him to stand up again. "I heard you crying!"

"Oh." His mother frowned, mouth pursed into a tight line. "I must have knocked the button on my mobile, I didn't know…"

Flora looked away from Zac and his mother, feeling uncomfortable. Zac's father's eyes flashed with pure hatred when they met her gaze. She shrank away backwards into the corridor, feeling nauseous again.

I really shouldn't have come…

She could still hear their voices from the hallway.

"Why don't you leave, mum?" Zac's voice was entreating. "Come away with me now. Just leave and let me take care of you."

Then she heard a roar and shouting in French and she guessed

Zac's dad had decided he'd had enough of sitting quietly. She heard the word 'quittez' and knew enough French to guess he was saying Zac should be the one to leave, ordering him to get out of his house.

"I'm not a little boy anymore, Dad." Zac raised his voice but didn't shout. "You can't beat me into submission anymore."

"He's always tried to be a good father to you, Zachary." His mother's voice rose to join in.

Flora walked towards the front door as quietly as she could, feeling winded and wishing she could literally disappear. It was all too much to deal with. She felt for Zac, really she did but she didn't know what to do. Presumably no one would thank her if she called the police and Zac's mum would refuse to make a complaint.

"Please mum." Zac's voice was still audible when Flora reached for the catch and opened the front door. A vice-like grip squeezed her chest and she could barely breathe, as though even her lungs were afraid of being heard.

She walked to Zac's Jeep and stood with her back against it, watching the house, her fingers twisting anxiously together.

Zac emerged from the house, his face blank of all emotion although his eyes were grim.

I don't know what to say…

"I'm sorry," she said simply, her eyes annoyingly deciding to choose that moment to fill with tears. "I'm so sorry."

What's she sorry about? Sorry but she has to dash, has remembered she needs to be back at Chalet Repos? Sorry she can't do this anymore…what?

What had happened back at the house must have been awful for her. Worse than that, she'd seen him hit a man, an elderly man at that…she must think he was as bad as her ex.

Maybe I am… What kind of a person must she think I am? But she has no idea what's happened, the things he's done to mum over the years, is still doing.

How could he tell her all that stuff? He never talked about it and wasn't sure he had the emotional vocabulary. It was much easier when he was trying to cheer Flora up, trying to help her… he didn't feel comfortable with the situation reversed.

He opened his mouth to speak but nothing came out. He put the key into the ignition, desperate to put some distance between the house and them, wishing he'd never brought Flora here. It might have worked if his dad had answered the door, he would've had time to assume his usual act. But when they hadn't answered the door there'd been no choice, he'd had to use his old key.

Zac put the Jeep in gear and drove off a little too fast, gravel crunching beneath the tyres, spraying up into the bushes.

Should he tell Flora it had only been the second time he'd ever hit anyone in his life? The first time he'd hit his dad he'd been eighteen and he'd moved out straight away afterwards, paying his own way through university with as many part time jobs as he could manage on top of his studies.

But if I had a franc for every time I wish I'd hit him I'd be far richer than he is. Doesn't that make me just as bad as him?

"Zac, are you okay there?" Flora placed a gentle hand on his thigh, bringing him back from the dark thoughts swirling round in his mind. He only realised he'd been holding his breath when he heard himself sigh at her touch.

"I'll be fine," he replied shortly. He wasn't fine, but he would be. He planned to be. That was how it usually worked. If you worked hard enough at it, nothing needed to keep you down forever. Flora didn't need his crap dumped on her, however tempting it might be to just let go.

He paused at the junction and turned to look at her. Actually she looked terrible, her face as pale as a ghost.

"If you'd rather I took you back to Chalet Repos instead of to the Mirador I'll understand. I could always bring your bags over… or…" Zac tried to keep all his emotions in check. He didn't want her to go, he needed her right now, needed another human body to be close to. He needed someone who understood.

He needed Flora but that was selfish. What about what she needed?

His throat felt tight and painful, like he'd swallowed sandpaper.

"No." She lifted her hand from his thigh and he felt the loss of the contact. "Unless you wanted me to, you know, go? Did you want to be on your own?"

Out of the corner of his eye Zac saw her lip tremble and he pulled over into a lay-by. He undid his seatbelt and took her in his arms. She burst into tears, burying her head against his shoulder.

He stroked her back, feeling the pressure to contain his own emotions. She needed looking after, so he had to squash his own issues down. That was just how it went.

It was how it had always been.

"I need you to know Flora, what you saw… I would never hit a woman!" He whispered into her hair. "I had to stop him, I had to…"

"Hey I understand, really I do." She turned curious eyes up to his face, looking a little confused. "Sorry, I'm just a bit… stressed, you know?"

"Yep, there's a lot of it going around," he replied.

"I know. Look, he wouldn't come after us would he? He really didn't seem to like me very much." She glanced anxiously over his shoulder as though half expecting his father to drive up behind them.

"He wouldn't take me on now. Bullies only pick on those weaker than themselves, they don't like a fair fight." Zac's tone was flat. It was as though someone had sucked all of the emotions out of him, leaving him cold as ice.

For the umpteenth time he cursed himself for bringing Flora along. He'd ruined whatever they had going on and just as he was beginning to well, feel something.

"Not exactly the best Christmas, eh?" he put the Jeep into gear again and indicated to pull out.

"It never is as perfect as we hope, is it?" Flora stared out of the passenger window and didn't replace her hand on his leg. He sensed the shift in her was more than physical.

She might be sympathetic but she'd withdrawn from him and he felt the growing gap between them.

Had he stuffed this up?

"Tom hit me," Flora blurted out and Zac fought to keep his concentration on the road, his natural instinct being to turn back to her.

"Oh?" He glanced over, startled and then had to turn his attention back to the road when someone hooted their horn behind them.

"Only once," her eyes were downcast and her fingers twisting in her lap. "Well it was twice really. I should've left after the first time but you know… it's never quite the same when you're in the situation yourself. You know the advice you'd give your friends if anyone ever hit them and you think you know how you'd react… but real life is always so much messier and more complicated and Tom wasn't all bad. If he had been all bad it would have been so much easier to go."

Her voice had dropped to a whisper and Zac regretted having pulled the car back out into the road, now there was nowhere to pull in. But maybe she needed him to be driving in the same way she'd need it to be dark in the bedroom before she'd open herself up to him.

"You did the right thing." The words left his lips instinctively. "There was no way you could have stayed and no way anyone in their right mind would expect you to. No one who cared about you would've wanted you to stay in that situation."

So why won't mum leave? I really can't understand it. I've said I'll take care of her. We can manage without… him.

Zac thought he might be choking with the pain of it. He took a deep breath to restore his calm and the crisis passed.

"Do you think your mother will leave?" Flora asked, making him start. How had she done that? How had she read his mind?

Zac took another deep breath. "At first they were staying together because of me, supposedly. Now there's no other reason than that he's become her world, her provider, her everything…"

"Maybe she loves him," Flora suggested tentatively. "Maybe she loves him despite everything. I know it must be really, really hard to stomach but it's her choice and you can't make her leave."

"I know," he replied, his voice taut and his control cracking. But did he know? Really? Hadn't he been trying to force his wishes on his mother for years? And if so then wasn't that an indication that he liked to be in control too?

He didn't trust himself to say anymore. He put his foot on the accelerator and headed for the autoroute to take them back to Vevey and the Mirador. Maybe things would feel better when they were back there. Perhaps they could hit the rewind button and just take up where they'd left off, as though none of this had ever happened.

Yeah right! And I'll get a call to say mum has left dad and he's really sorry for all the stuff he's done wrong. Life simply doesn't happen like that Zac, haven't you figured that out yet?

If he was like his dad then maybe it was a good thing he'd never committed to a relationship. Maybe this was why he'd been avoiding emotional entanglements. Had he been afraid a relationship might disintegrate into the kind of scenes he'd witnessed growing up? After all it was so much safer to be single, no one to argue with, no one he needed to protect.

It wasn't fair to make Flora witness more scenes like that one this morning after all she'd been through. It'd clearly really shaken her. And he was never going to give up his mum, so… Flora didn't need this kind of hassle. He was going to have to do the decent thing.

Even though the decent thing stunk to high heaven.

But the fear he might not be able to protect Flora hammered away in his chest. He couldn't even protect his mum so how would he be able to shield Flora as well? His muscles were still taut with tension and although he tried to smile when they got back to their hotel suite he knew it wasn't very convincing.

Suddenly he was tired. So very, very tired.

They ordered from room service and ate in silence. Zac thought he would've preferred the sounds of other diners around them compared to this pregnant silence. When Flora had finished she yawned widely, covering her mouth with her hand. "Do you mind if we just go to sleep? I'm shattered."

It looked like she was going to make things easy for him. His original plan had been to keep this thing with Flora as a holiday fling with a question mark ending.

There was no question mark now.

He'd end it after the wedding. It would be awkward to finish it before and then bump into each other and Christmas Day had been bad enough already without adding to it.

Not that he really wanted to end it at all. Still. An unutterable weariness weighed down his limbs with the knowledge of 'The Right Thing'.

I can't put Flora through another scene like today.

"Are you sure you're okay, after, you know, everything?" Zac asked as they climbed into the pristine white bed that had been made up by housekeeping in their absence. He tossed the complimentary chocolate and weather forecast card from his pillow onto the bedside cabinet and sank gratefully into bed.

"Yes, sure," Flora replied, she snuggled up to him but felt tense in his arms. He ached to make love to her but he knew he had to back off. She'd practically told him to hadn't she? Or maybe she was simply knackered? He knew he was.

I'm too tired to read subtext. I wish women came with subtext subtitles or at the very least always said exactly what they mean. It would make life so much easier.

It didn't feel fair to make love to her now he'd decided to end it, anyway. For all her bravado, Flora clearly wasn't used to casual sex and he really didn't want to hurt her. He longed to protect her, not to add to the pain she'd already had to deal with.

The best way you can protect Flora is to stay well away from her. If you stay around you're going to be constantly opening up old wounds. What happens the next time you get a call from mum? Because there's going to be a next time.

There always was.

"So, what time do you want me to drop you off at Chalet Repos in the morning?" he asked causally, wanting to take the words back as soon as they'd left his lips.

But he couldn't.

And why delay the inevitable? It was like taking off a plaster – best to do it quick and get the pain over and done with.

She tensed next to him. "Of course, if you've got stuff to do tomorrow, I should be getting back anyway, I promised Holly I'd help with wedding prep. Will I, er, see you at the wedding?"

"Of course. We can go together if you like?" Zac knew he'd detonated a land mine. He'd chosen to press the self-destruct button on the best thing to happen to him in years.

And only the sense he was doing the right thing stopped him pulling Flora to him and demonstrating exactly how special he thought she was.

It was for the best.

So why did it feel so utterly wrong?

CHAPTER SIX

Misery weighed Flora down as she lay at Zac's side. She might be inexperienced but she knew a brush off when she saw one. She wasn't stupid. Only now he was cutting her loose did she realise just how much she wanted him to go on being a part of her life.

How could she blame him? She'd been the one to put a best-before date of New Year's Eve on the relationship after all. Not that she'd told him about it, obviously.

So she shouldn't be angry to find out he'd done exactly the same thing and was calling time on the fling/shag/relationship, whatever it was. Delete as appropriate. Who knew what label he'd put on it?

But she was – pissed off and miserable. This Christmas break had started out so perfectly she'd begun to dream about all sorts of things she'd promised herself she wouldn't.

It felt awful, unnatural even, to be so close to Zac and yet not be making love. Her body still tingled at the memory of how he'd last made her feel. She'd even let him go down on her and hadn't felt stressed about the intimacy. That had to be a good sign, right?

She sighed, turning over and pulling her legs up to her chest to lie in the foetal position. Zac's hand lightly stroked her back and she tensed, hoping for more, even though she'd said she just wanted to sleep. She'd said that because she was stressed out, not because she hadn't wanted Zac…

Today had been emotion overload and she couldn't handle any more right now.

But then he withdrew his hand. She stared at the wall, longing for his touch but too proud to ask for it this time and convinced she'd never get to sleep.

She must have been more exhausted than she realised from all the emotional fall out of the day because the next thing she knew sunlight was streaming through the windows, lighting the room with a pale golden glow.

So, that was it. Christmas was over and so were she and Zac. At least they were as good as. A wedding date was just going through the motions, being polite. He was, if nothing else, a gentleman.

Although, sod that, he was a hell of a lot more than a gentleman and after what she'd seen yesterday she admired him all the more for emerging from his home life as unscathed as he had.

He was strong, one of life's survivors, and something in her was drawn to that. She liked it when he held her, she felt safe.

Oh God, she was going to cry again and she hadn't even got out of bed yet. She pinched the bridge of her nose. If Zac could manage yesterday's crap with such grace then she wasn't going to let the side down again. It wasn't fair of her to be constantly breaking down on him. She might not be a shrink but even she could see where Zac's desire to care and protect came from.

But who looks after him?

A desire to be there for him mounted inside her, tears welling in her eyes again without warning. It was so sad to think of Zac as a boy, growing up with a dad like that and a mum who always put the dad first. She wanted to shout at his parents to bloody well appreciate the son they'd been given and get their messed up heads in order.

It wouldn't help the situation but it would make her feel a hell of a lot better.

She rolled onto her back and blinked back the tears.

Think happy thoughts, Flora. Think about the wedding, how happy Holly is and how good she and Scott have been to you. Think about hitting the slopes, drinking in mountain canteens and endless days of sunshine...

For some reason that led her to thinking about sex with Zac – how alive and affirmed she'd felt by it. She'd miss the sex. She'd miss Zac.

He didn't look much better than she felt and they barely spoke as they dressed and packed their bags to check out. Flora took one last look at the perfect view over the lake to the Alps and swallowed down the bitter disappointment. She'd been so happy when they'd checked in. When had she last been that happy?

She could barely look at Zac for fear she'd blurt out something really embarrassing or start crying or something. She managed a few lines about the wedding and what Scott and Holly were planning for the ceremony but beyond that the drive back to Verbier was a quiet one. Flora pretended to be looking out at the scenery every time tears threatened to leak out. She really hoped he hadn't noticed. She had to act cool. That was what you were supposed to do in these situations, right? Well she was going to have to get used to it. She'd have to toughen up a bit. Or become a recluse, which was always an option.

Zac didn't say much. She guessed he must still be upset about what had happened at his parents yesterday. If she'd needed a reminder of why she was doing this whole independence thing then the incident had been perfectly timed.

So, this was the right thing. Being single. Protecting herself.

For the right thing it sure hurt.

She lurched over from the passenger seat to kiss Zac on the cheek as soon as they pulled up outside Chalet Repos, needing to get the goodbye over and done with quickly. That way she might just might manage to avoid making a twat of herself.

"Thanks so much for the hotel and everything, you know... it's been fun," she said.

It had been so much more than fun. She'd experienced the kind of connection she hadn't even realised existed with Zac and yet still she was walking away.

Life could be fricking complicated.

And she had to remember he was the one giving her the brush off. So that meant, according to dating rules as she'd understood them from the safety of a long-term relationship, she had to act coolly and pretend that it was her idea.

Which actually it kind of had been to start with.

Oh hell!

She had a tension headache from all the repressed tears. As soon as they'd mumbled a goodbye and awkwardly kissed cheeks like the friends they were now destined to be, she fled into Chalet Repos' back entrance, unable to bear looking back at the car and Zac. Silent tears dripped down her cheeks as she stumbled to the bathroom, the only room in Chalet Repos with a lock and some privacy. But in the corridor she bumped into Holly.

"Hello stranger!" Holly smiled and then her eyes widened as she saw Flora's face. "Hey, what's up?"

"I… I…" Flora stammered, unable to form anything resembling a sentence. She glanced over Holly's shoulder, aware that anyone might come down the corridor and overhear them.

"Let's go to the storeroom." Holly took Flora's elbow and steered her gently down to the basement. "Sometimes I go there for a bit of peace and quiet myself."

"Oh?" Flora choked back her sobs. "I'm… so… sorry Holly."

"Don't be sorry. Cry as much as you need to. But tell me what's wrong and we'll see if we can sort it, okay?"

Holly's soothing, no-nonsense tones helped calm Flora. They entered the storeroom and once the door was shut Flora let her guard down, slumping onto a crate. Holly sat down next to her and placed a hand over hers.

It was just the right amount of bodily contact – enough for Flora to know she wasn't as utterly alone as she felt. Holly didn't speak, just waited quietly next to her and her patience soothed Flora's strained nerves.

"It's been a weird couple of days..." Flora found her story coming out. Not all of it, she didn't think it was right to share the details of what had happened at Zac's parents, that was his secret to tell.

"How do you know he doesn't think *you* wanted to end it?" Holly asked when Flora had finished. "Some people jump before they're pushed you know?"

"I suppose." Flora fell silent, thinking about Zac. It had all been going great until Christmas Day and the thing with his parents.

"Did you even give him any indication you really liked him and wanted to carry on seeing him?" Holly asked, rocking back on her crate.

"Of course not." Flora almost smiled. "And risk being humiliated?"

"Could you really feel any worse than you do right now?" Holly fixed her gaze on Flora.

"You've got a point." Flora sighed.

"If you only listen to one thing I say today then make it this – be open with him. Zac's one of the good guys." Holly patted Flora's hand. "I like him, I think he's worth fighting for. You could do a lot worse. Well from the sound of it you already have done a lot worse..."

"You're right there." Flora grimaced.

Holly stared at her, her eyes thoughtful, as though debating something internally. "You know it wasn't all plain sailing with me and Scott getting together?"

"Really? But you're perfect together." Flora turned towards Holly, surprised.

"Sometimes you just have to take a leap of faith. Particularly when you're a survivor. Having bad stuff happen to you makes it harder but it doesn't make it impossible," Holly said. "We obsess so much about timing or what we should be doing but really – if something good comes along in this life I say you need to grab it with both hands and hold onto it. Otherwise you're living a life of fear and that's really not much fun."

Staring into Holly's eyes Flora knew that her boss really knew what it was like to have her life implode. She understood.

"How did you get so wise?" she asked.

Holly shrugged. "Life happened. But let's think practically. A bit of breathing space might be a good idea and I've got a few things that could take your mind off it, if you wouldn't mind helping with some last minute wedding prep? I've been having a bit of a problem with organising the urns for the Glühwein to help the guests keep warm while we're in the chapel. As you know it's so tiny we're not all going to fit in for the first bit."

"Hey, I'd love to help. It's the least I can do to repay you for the pep talk!"

"Well, anytime you need pepping, I'm your woman." Holly patted Flora on the back. "Ready to face the masses? I warn you Scott's parents are a little, erm, stuffy so I'd steer clear of them. But don't tell him I said that. You know what it's like, we criticise our own parents all the time but no one else is allowed to do it!"

"Sure." Flora smiled and followed Holly out of the storeroom, not feeling better exactly but certainly a lot calmer.

It was time to stop lying to herself and grow up a bit. She had something special with Zac, a connection she'd never experienced with Tom. And to let that go because of some misguided notion that she ought to be single for a bit was madness.

She was going to fight for Zac. Even if he said no and didn't feel the same way at least she'd know she'd given it her best shot.

But there was something else she needed to do first.

Flora saw Zac before he saw her. She put her skis into the rack, not wanting to be encumbered and needing a moment to get her thoughts together before she went for it. It was such a fun idea of Holly's for them to all ski, board or skidoo down from the tiny chapel. Those outside the chapel would be able to warm themselves with glasses of Glühwein before the whole party made its way down to the canteen for a Swiss food extravaganza of raclette, fondue and rösti.

It was certainly very different from the traditional wedding she'd planned with Tom. It was as though she'd been a completely different person back then, not even knowing her own preferences, so anxious was she to keep everyone happy. She barely recognised herself.

Holly and Scott were having their wedding the way they wanted it, despite the grumbling from Scott's parents. Good on them.

All the preparations for the wedding day were done and Flora was glad she'd been around to help. But now it was time to do something nice for herself.

"Hi there," she called out. He turned, eyes lighting up with recognition.

It felt like coming home.

"Hi there." His smile reached his eyes and she wanted to kiss him.

Talking first, kissing second.

"How are you?" She walked over to him, feeling her heart beating hard in her ribcage.

Be brave!

"I'm, er, great."

He didn't look great. Sure he looked super hot as per usual but his eyes were bloodshot and tiredness was etched into his face. Had he not been sleeping?

Is it conceited to think I might be the cause? Go on Flora, it's the only way you'll ever know. Holly was right – who wants to live a life full of regrets?

"I really like you, Zac," she blurted out, too nervous to begin her preprepared speech. It was hard to remember her lines now she was actually standing here, taking a chance.

"I like you too, but…" He shook his head.

"Ssh." She placed a finger on his lips before he could go on and, softly he kissed it, his eyes gleaming. Now she knew for sure she was doing the right thing. "Let me say what I've got to say first, please?"

He nodded.

"I'd like us to start seeing each other," she said. "No wishy-washy, vague flings or friends with benefits. I think we have something special and we shouldn't throw that away, for any reason."

Zac shook his head again, slowly, sadly. Staring into his eyes she saw real anguish.

"Why don't you just tell me what's wrong?" She reached out a hand to touch the sleeve of his ski jacket, as though trying to keep him anchored to her. The sun had disappeared behind a cloud and the cold wind from the snow covered Alps chilled her. What if this didn't work after all? "Everything was fine, well it was more than fine, until Christmas Day at your…"

"Exactly. My parents. I don't think it's fair to put you through that again Flora. You need to be well away from… well I saw how much that day affected you." He stared at her imploringly, his eyes begging her to understand. He gently stroked the side of her face, his fingers were warm against her cold skin. "You were as white as a sheet that day and it was my fault for taking you there. I can't expose you to that again."

"Hey, isn't that my decision to make?" she asked softly. "And don't I remember you giving me a lecture about not taking responsibility for other people's actions? What happened that day was your father's fault. End of."

She was dimly aware of the people around them, gathering to ski or board to the chapel together. But all that mattered to her was Zac and at the moment she didn't give a fig what anyone thought of her, either here in Verbier or back home in England.

This was her world, right here with Zac, the world she was making.

"But, the thing is, it doesn't seem fair to you… after you've escaped that kind of relationship. You see I'm never going to stop wanting to look out for my mum so I can't promise what happened will never happen again, you know?" Zac sighed heavily, the weariness from the previous nights clear in his face.

She wanted to soothe away the stress and let him sleep in her arms. She wanted to make things okay for him. Could she? Would he at least let her try?

"I wouldn't expect you to. You don't need to worry about me. I can look after myself, hey I can even look after you when you need it. It's not a one way street." She planted a soft kiss on his lips and then buried her head on his chest, not even knowing how the distance between them had closed. "We can look after each other."

"What if I turn out to be… like him," Zac said in a low voice. With one ear against his chest she could hear his heart beating, it was kind of comforting. "You must have thought I was like your ex when you saw what happened with my Dad."

"No! You had to stop him." She pulled her face away from Zac's chest to stare at him. "How can you even think that? I'd have done the same. You are nothing like my ex and nothing like your dad from the little I've seen of him, which was enough. Look I have something to show you."

She pulled her phone out of her pocket. "Look!"

Scrolling down the screen she showed him the few listings she had on Etsy for the bags she already had made and had pictures uploaded. "I went through that paperwork you gave me and I've made a start."

"I thought you hated me sticking my nose in." Zac raised an eyebrow.

"I kind of did. At first anyway," she admitted. "It pushed my buttons, you know, having someone telling me what to do… But I've realised what the main difference is between you and men like my ex and your Dad – they only ever try to belittle the women in their lives, to make themselves feel bigger. Whereas you… you do the opposite. I've been stupid, okay? Stupid and scared."

He pulled her into a hug but she held her face away, maintaining eye contact. This had to be said and she needed to know he was listening.

"You want to help me. You're trying to build me up. That's why you'll never be like… them." She wiped the stray tears escaping from her eyes. "Oh no, I'm sorry, I appear to be leaking again! Do you think we could stop talking and you could kiss me? That usually seems to fix it."

"I thought you simply walked up to guys you wanted to kiss and went for it. Isn't that the way you usually operate?" The corners of his mouth twitched and his eyes crinkled in amusement, teasing affection replacing his previously haunted expression.

She glowered at him and he grinned at her outraged expression.

Then he dropped his mouth to hers and they kissed. With all the doubts bulldozed away her body filled with pure, unmitigated joy. No guilt. No shame.

No regrets.

She never knew kissing could be this good and didn't want it to stop. She clung to him and ignored the wolf whistles from the crowd around them. This time she didn't give a stuff.

When they eventually pulled apart she whispered in his ear. "Want to play Truth or Dare with me?"

She did have something prepared, this was part of her script, but now she was here in front of Zac she worried he might find it a bit cheesy.

"My Truth is I think I'm falling in love with you, Flora." He held her face in his hands and although he'd ruined her lines she loved that he got it, that he'd even copied her speech idea without realising. "My Dare is I dare to trust you."

"And your Forfeit?" she asked, holding her breath.

"Well… My Forfeit is… Wait, I've got it, I want to forfeit being single. I want there to be an 'us' instead of just a 'me.' What do you think?"

His usually confident expression wavered a little, a hint of vulnerability had crept into his eyes and it made her love him all the more.

"And you, what's your Truth?" Zac's grin was infectious. Flora's own mouth stretched into a wide smile.

"Well my Truth is I think I love you too." She giggled, deciding not to care if her lines were cheesy, she meant them. "And my Dare is to take a leap of faith with you."

"Oh, what sort of leap?" The corners of his lips twitched. "Will you let me teach you to snowboard?"

"Maybe." She shrugged and, in an attempt to casually lean back, managed to lose her footing on the snow, sinking down into an unexpectedly deep patch. She reached out to grab his sleeve and deliberately pulled him over with her into the drift. She got the giggles as they tumbled onto the ground next to each other.

"And what do you Forfeit?" He murmured in her ear, brushing some snow out of her hair. "Other than your sanity, which you've clearly lost already."

"Oi, you," She swatted him. "I'm merely proving to you I don't care what other people think any more. My Forfeit is… me. I give you me."

She snuggled up against him, pressing into his body, suddenly not feeling cold anymore.

He groaned. "I'm quite happy with that Forfeit."

Even through their thick layers of clothing her body responded to him, darts of excitement and anticipation finding their targets. She didn't care about the whistles or calls to 'Get a room' from those around them. She could have laid like that for ages, the snowfall was fresh and powdery, making a comfortable bed. But then her gaze fell onto Zac's watch.

"Help! We need to get going. Hold that thought for the moment." She got up to her feet and reached out her hand to him. "Let's get my skis and your snowboard. We've got a wedding to go to."

The End

Don't miss the first in Lorraine Wilson's Chalet Girls series, *Confessions of a Chalet Girl* available now!